Flames of Flamenco

by

Jennifer Ivy Walker

Flames of Flamenco

Cover Art by *Rae Monet, Inc.*

The Wild Rose Press, Inc.
PO Box 708
Adams Basin, NY 14410-0708
Visit us at www.thewildrosepress.com

Publishing History
First Edition, 2023
Trade Paperback ISBN 978-1-5092-5251-0
Digital ISBN 978-1-5092-5250-3

Published in the United States of America

Dedication

To Ana, my steadfast, supportive friend.

For all the chills that ran up your arms every time I told you about this passionate story.

Other Wild Rose Press Titles by Jennifer Ivy Walker:

The Wild Rose and the Sea Raven
The Lady of the Mirrored Lake
The Emerald Fairy and the Dragon Knight
Winter Solstice in the Crystal Castle

Chapter 1

Montmartre

Ella strolled along the cobbled stone square of *Montmartre,* the bohemian heart of Paris nestled behind the famous white church, *le Sacré-Coeur.* A sultry jazz melody from a smooth saxophone floated among the red and white striped umbrellas, the bright streetlamps, and the canopy of manicured trees under the starry night sky.

Meandering among the tourists getting their portraits sketched on the chic and trendy *Place du Tertre,* she inhaled the invigorating, intoxicating *mélange* of scents. Decadent chocolate crêpes. Sizzling seafood. Strong French coffee.

An American teacher of French from Florida, Ella had won a summer scholarship to come to Paris and practice her language skills through the study of art in Montmartre. For the glorious month of June, she would be residing near *la Maison Rose*, a restaurant once frequented by such artists as Picasso and Dali. She'd be taking French language and culture classes with other teachers from around the world, their linguistic learning enhanced through workshops in various *ateliers* by local painters and sculptors.

Ella had arrived a few days early, before the academic program began, to allow herself sufficient time to explore Paris on her own, thrilled at the chance for a new beginning.

She'd finally divorced the husband who had ignored her for years, leaving her feeling undesirable, unattractive, and unwanted. Ella had applied for the scholarship, never expecting that she would be one of twenty-four teachers selected. And now, here she was. In Paris, The City of Light. *La Ville Lumière.*

With a deep intake of breath, she clutched the teal leather purse where her stamped passport was tucked safely inside its zippered pouch. And plunged headfirst into the adventurous, welcoming night.

As she wandered among the tourists, watching profiles emerge on canvas, deciding who she would choose to sketch her portrait as a souvenir for this most memorable summer, one artist caught her eye.

And took her breath away.

Thick, glossy, black hair cascaded down his back. Sinuous tattoos snaked up either side of his muscular neck, slithering from beneath the snug black tee-shirt molded to the sculpted biceps of his long, athletic arms. A mustache and several days' worth of dark stubble joined the trim beard which outlined his chiseled jawline and clefted chin.

A ripple of desire shivered up Ella's spine.

He must have sensed her watching him, for he looked up from his work to gaze across *la Place du Tertre.*

Their eyes met, and Ella was transfixed.

An irresistible aura of mystery and passion exuded from his every pore. He flashed her a glorious, dazzling grin.

Her knees nearly buckled from the blinding impact.

Stunned—for she was unused to male attention, let

alone captivating charm—it took a moment before she smiled back. *I want him to sketch me. And melt me with that scorching smile.*

Ella strode toward him, taking her place in line behind the three other tourists awaiting their turn to be sketched. She watched him work, awed by his artistic skill, nimble fingers coaxing lifelike images to appear miraculously on the smooth white paper affixed to the canvas on his easel. Thumbing through some of his pieces for sale on an adjacent stand, Ella discovered a small painting of a flamenco dancer that called to her, stirring the creative depths of her inner soul.

The tiered ruffles of the form-fitting red dress cascaded from delicate fingers of the elegant arm curled up over the dancer's retracted head. A sleek, black bun graced the nape of her neck, her slender throat sensuously exposed over her bent, arched back. The thumb and forefinger of her other hand formed a circle near her curved waist, the long fingers unfurling like wings of an exquisite swan.

But it was the agony and ecstasy in the dancer's intense facial expression that gripped Ella's heart. The passion and pain. The joy and despair. The savage beauty and ethereal grace. Ella had to have this painting. *Was this dancer his lover? Is that why she is so intimately portrayed?*

Surprised at the personal train of her thoughts, Ella realized it was her turn to be sketched. She stumbled forward, presented the painting to the artist, and spluttered, "I'd like to purchase this, in addition to having my portrait sketched."

He grinned broadly, his handsome, stubbled face aglow with pleasure. "We share similar tastes. That's one of my favorites as well."

When he took the painting from her hand, his calloused fingers brushed against hers, sending a delicious wave of heat up Ella's arm. As she watched him lovingly wrap the small canvas in white paper, she glimpsed an intriguing tattoo—an abstract image of a flamenco dancer— on his prominent right bicep.

Her treasure tucked safely into a paper shopping bag, he handed her the parcel with a satisfied smile. "*Merci beaucoup*. Please, sit here for your portrait."

Ella settled onto the folding chair provided for his patrons, glad she had worn a clingy mauve halter top which flattered her lithe form. As she crossed her bare legs, his appreciative eyes roved over her long limbs, a hunger in his lingering gaze that Ella had never glimpsed in her disinterested, inattentive husband.

A delicious thrill rippled up Ella's spine.

She pulled a strand of long blonde hair forward over her shoulder. Proud of the length—it touched her waist—she wanted him to capture it in the sketch. Ready for him to begin, she looked up to meet his eyes.

And lost herself in the smoldering, dark depths. Decadent and delicious as French chocolate. A wave of warmth melted her inner core.

"Lift your torso and tilt your head slightly to the left. Look at me. And smile."

As she complied, Ella found herself enthralled by the bohemian artist whose torn, faded jeans hugged his sculpted, muscular thighs.

With a sultry grin, he chuckled. "As much as I appreciate your roaming eyes—and believe me, I do— I need you to look at me so I can capture you on canvas."

Ella felt her face flush as she returned her gaze to his

striking face. She imagined the full, sensuous lips parting and sampling her own.

And sucking her breasts.

Her nipples tingled, and from the glint in his eyes, he'd noticed the protruding tips which clamored for attention. *He has such a powerful effect on me… I'm glad he can't read my thoughts. Or can he?*

As she sat still in the chair, holding the required pose, his impassioned eyes flitted from her face to the canvas, his adroit fingers invoking their magic. Each stroke of charcoal felt like a caress upon her skin, as if he were making love to her through his art.

Legs trembling under her short denim skirt, the rhythmic throbbing and mounting tension between her thighs was becoming increasingly difficult to ignore.

"You are exquisite." The deep timbre of his melodic voice strummed her like a harp. "You have such beautiful hair. Long and lustrous…" the charcoal stick slid sensuously in his skilled hand. "Most French women prefer short styles. But I love long hair… like yours." Another dazzling smile washed her in a luxurious wave of lust.

Ella nearly fell off her chair.

"Thank you." Her voice quavered as she adjusted her legs, balancing her feet against the cobbled stone pavement.

"Look at me and lift your chin. Tilt your head a bit. *Voilà.* Just like that. I'm almost finished."

Breathless with anticipation, Ella's mouth dropped open when he proudly displayed the completed portrait. It was her, but she looked… beautiful. Exotic. Alluring.

He'd captured her long hair, her slender arms, and the sensuous longing in her sultry gaze. With incredible, artistic magic.

She slid off the chair and approached for a better look. He'd glimpsed her soul. And captured it on canvas.

Ella was astounded. "It's magnificent. I love it! Thank you so much."

"You are most welcome." One side of his full mouth curled upward, his dark eyes glinting in the starlight. He placed a sheet of protective paper over the charcoal portrait, rolled it up, and tucked it into the shopping bag alongside the other small painting of the flamenco dancer.

Ella gave him her debit card. He swiped it and held it out for the signature.

"I'd like to paint you," he murmured as she signed her name. "To portray the intriguing blend of shyness on the surface...and the smoldering passion hidden underneath." Desire danced in his dark eyes. "How long are you staying in Paris?"

Ella gulped. He wanted to paint her? The smoldering passion beneath her shy surface? Maybe he had read her lusty thoughts after all. "For the month of June," she stammered, smoothing the sides of her skirt to wipe her sweaty palms.

"Excellent." He handed her his business card. "My name is Jean-Luc Cortés. What's yours?"

"Ella Jacobs." She searched his face, trembling at the thought of being alone with him in his studio. Of having him *capture her smoldering passion*. Desire throbbed between her long legs.

"Are you free tomorrow? My *atelier* is close by. Are you staying here in Montmartre?"

"Yes, in a *résidence* near *la Maison Rose.*"

Jean-Luc glanced around *la Place du Tertre*. A few

tourists were still getting their portraits sketched, but for the most part, it was quiet. "I have no more customers tonight. And I'm starving. Would you like to get something to eat? Maybe see a show? I'll bring you back here afterwards and walk you safely home."

How different from Florida, where everything closes at nine. Here in Paris, you can go to a restaurant and see a show at all hours. Positively exhilarating! Thrilled at the thought of spending more time with Jean-Luc—as a desirable woman rather than a paying customer—Ella whispered enthusiastically, "I'd love that!"

White teeth flashed in his dark, handsome face. "I know a local *tablao* where they serve delicious *paella*, and we can watch a flamenco performance." Gesturing to the bag in her hand, he remarked, "You loved my painting, *La Alma.* That's the essence of flamenco. The *soul* of the music expressed through the passion of dance. I think you'll love the show."

"I'm sure I will." Ella inhaled deeply, the magic of the night bewitching. Beguiling. Beckoning.

Jean-Luc packed up his art supplies, loaded them into a box, and carefully stacked the unsold paintings. "I'll leave the chairs and the display stand here, but I'll bring these back to my studio. Come with me and I'll show you where it is as I drop these off." He cautiously placed the box of supplies and stack of paintings in a large sack. "That way, you'll know where to come tomorrow. Say… around one or two? I give art lessons in the morning, but I'm free in the afternoon. Is that a good time for you?"

"Yes, that's perfect. You give art lessons? I'm a teacher, too. A French teacher from Florida. I'm here on a scholarship. To perfect my language skills as I learn about art in Montmartre." Ella smiled as he slung the supply bag over a broad shoulder.

With a heart-melting grin, Jean-Luc replied, "You can practice both on me."

Heat flared in her lonely loins at the thought of *practicing* on Jean-Luc. She swallowed a lump of desire.

And remembered to breathe.

"*Allez, viens.* My *atelier* is this way." With a nod of his head and another dazzling smile, Jean-Luc indicated the direction, and Ella crossed the cobbled stone square of *la Place du Tertre* beside the handsome Parisian artist who made her heart sing for the first time in many years.

They strolled down a picturesque side street and arrived at a studio where Venetian blinds covered the glass front display window. Above the blue painted wooden door, Ella spotted the name *"Atelier des Lumières"* and another sign—*Fermé*—indicating that the shop was closed. Jean-Luc unlocked the door, turned on the light, and led her inside while he placed his bag of supplies and unsold paintings on a large table in the corner.

Ella glanced around the bright, vibrant room where numerous paintings covered the sunny, lemon-yellow walls. *Atelier des Lumières. Studio of Lights. The perfect name for a bohemian artist in Paris.*

A set of wooden stairs led up to a second story above the workshop. "I live in the apartment upstairs. It's perfect. I pay one rent, which covers my *atelier* and my residence. Convenient and affordable. Well, nothing in Paris is truly affordable, but I get by." Obviously pleased that she was admiring his shop, he promised, "I'll show you more of my work tomorrow. And give you a proper tour." With a dashingly handsome grin, he offered her the crook of his elbow and suggested gallantly, "But now, let's get something to eat. And watch flamenco."

****

The *Tablao Flamenco* was housed on the hill of *Montmartre* inside an eighteenth century building whose façade had been redesigned to resemble a Spanish villa. The arched oval windows and wooden entrance door of the elegant white exterior were shaped like an Arabic mosque or Andalusian palace. Jean-Luc was warmly greeted by the staff—who obviously knew him well— and as the hostess led them down an arched, sloped entry into the dimly lit restaurant where the performance would be held, Ella was amazed that it felt like entering an underground cave.

Vibrant purple lights shone onto the elevated wooden stage at the center back of the cavernous chamber, the vivid color reflecting onto the white limestone walls and bathing the entire room in an astonishing plum hue. A golden glow glimmered from crystal lamps affixed to the arched stone side walls, gilding the lavender haze so that the entire establishment was like an iridescent, precious amethyst hidden like buried treasure inside a secret cave.

Waiters in white shirts and black pants carried trays of steaming *paella*, the sweet honey fragrance of saffron mingling with the tantalizing aroma of seafood and garlic, bustling among the packed, crowded round tables facing the stage.

"Voici votre table. Bon appétit. Et bon spectacle!" With a generous smile, the attractive brunette hostess escorted Jean-Luc and Ella to a small table for two and discreetly disappeared.

Jean-Luc gallantly seated Ella, then pulled his chair closer to hers as he settled down at her side. "Let's order a bottle of wine. Have you ever had *paella de marisco*? Seafood paella?"

A plaintive melody from a trio of acoustic guitars filled the room, the emotional, evocative notes stirring Ella's soul. *Jean-Luc described flamenco as la alma. The soul of the music. I feel it deep inside.* "No, I've never had *paella*, but I do love seafood," she replied as a competent waiter approached their table.

Jean-Luc ordered a bottle of *Meursault*—a dry white burgundy—to beautifully complement the exquisite flavors of the seafood, spices, and saffron.

When *le serveur* filled their glasses and left the bottle of *Meursault* in a bucket of ice on the table, Jean-Luc proposed a toast. "To your summer in Montmartre. May I show you all the sensual delights of Paris." The sultry timbre of Jean-Luc's deep baritone strummed a melody of flame in Ella's core, the mellow warmth from the rich, earthy wine a liquid fire in her veins.

The paella was bursting with the flavor of succulent mussels, spicy jumbo shrimp, red peppers, garlic, and saffron rice. Enhanced by the heady glow from the exquisite white burgundy, and the intensely attractive Jean-Luc at her side, Ella savored every delectable moment.

When they finished eating, the waiter cleared the table, refilling their wine glasses.

And the flamenco show began.

"The box that the musician is sitting on is called a *cajón*," Jean-Luc whispered in her ear as he pulled his chair closer to hers. His breath was hot against her cheek, the earthy scent of sumptuous wine enhancing the musky scent of healthy male. "He'll slap it in rhythm with the clapping. And the wooden stage is a percussive instrument as well, for it amplifies the dancers' intricate steps." He leaned closer, and Ella deeply inhaled the intoxicating, enticing blend of leather, spice, and virility that made her nipples tingle and liquid warmth flare between her quivering thighs.

Five female dancers—in alternating colors of red and yellow dresses with tiers of ruffles below the knee— sat upon chairs onstage as the trio of guitarists began playing a romantic tune. Five men dressed in black clapped in striking syncopation with the passionate music. As the tempo increased, the seated dancers clapped rhythmically, stomping their heeled shoes on the flat wooden stage.

The stone walls of the cave-like *tablao* were acoustically designed to amplify the sound of the performance, for the reverberations of the percussive stomping and clapping rumbled into Ella's very bones.

The dancers arose as one, their arms swooping in delicate arches over their heads, as their footsteps increased in speed and power, the thick heels of their black shoes like drumsticks frapping rhythmically against the smooth surface of the hard wooden floor. With elegance and grace, they picked up the hem of their dresses, the tiers of ruffles rippling as they spun, swirled, and stomped with passion, precision, and power.

Ella—a dancer at heart—was absolutely enthralled. Flamenco was pure passion. And she was engulfed in its fiery blaze.

When the show ended, Jean-Luc wiped a tear from Ella's cheek as he traced his fingers along the side of her face. He leaned forward and brushed his soft lips against her flushed skin. "I knew you would love it. And I'm pleased at how intensely it affected you." He hooked his finger under her chin and gently pulled her face to look at him. Ella swooned in the dark depths where desire danced like flickering flames. With full, sensuous lips, his soft kiss was a whisper of undiscovered delights. "Would you like to dance? I know a great club nearby."

Ella did not want the night to end. She longed to feel Jean-Luc's arms around her waist... his body moving against hers... "I would love that," she stammered, still brimming with emotion from the moving flamenco performance.

He rose to his feet and chivalrously extended his hand. As she placed her fingers inside his warm grasp, tremors of pleasure slipped up her arm. His eyes dipped to her breasts, where her erect nipples clamored for his touch. He dazzled her with that seductive smile, dark eyes ablaze with promised pleasure.

Ella rose to her feet on unsteady legs, gripping her bag of precious art. She had never been as attracted to any man as she was to Jean-Luc. Her entire body craved his touch. But so did her soul. After years of being ignored by a husband who had never loved her, Ella was starved for affection and attention.

Jean-Luc made her feel desirable.

And Ella hungered for more.

****

The dance club was packed. Amid flashing strobe lights, bodies swayed and pulsed to a visceral, thumping beat. Jean-Luc seated her at a small table and leaned forward, his full, curved lips close to her ear. "What would you like to drink?"

"A white Russian, please."

As Jean-Luc strode up to the bar, Ella watched several couples dancing on the crowded floor. Their limber bodies were pressed tightly together, the rhythmic thrusting explicitly suggestive. *I want Jean-Luc 's body against mine… just like that.*

He returned a few moments later with two glasses, handing one to her, as he pulled his chair closer. "I like this club. Haven't been here in a while." He sipped his drink as she did the same.

A song with a particularly catchy beat began, and Jean-Luc grabbed her hand and grinned. "C'mon. Let's dance."

Heady from the fabulous wine, feeling the buzz of the strong white Russian, Ella began moving to the beat as Jean-Luc's body molded to hers from behind.

He bared her shoulder, tossing her long blonde locks forward to one side, trailing his tongue and warm lips along her exposed neck. Heat throbbed in Ella's core, imagining his lips on her tingling nipples. Or the warm, wet ache between her quivering thighs.

Jean-Luc placed one palm possessively against her lower stomach, pinning her in place, his other hand gripping her hip, rolling her pelvis against his, in rhythm with the pulsing, pounding music.

As his hardened length pressed firmly into her backside, Ella rubbed the rigid tip of his cock with a shimmy of her denim-clad hips.

He was so tall that he leaned over her shoulder, wrapping one arm across the front of her hips, pressing his palm against her lower stomach, intensifying the aching throb between her weakened legs. His other hand stroked the side of her bare thigh, pulling her against him as he bent her forward, angling her upturned butt against his thickened body.

The rippled muscles of his abdomen were firm against her back, his irresistible hardness probing and prodding, seeking a way in.

If he hoists my skirt up a little higher, he can pull my panties to the side a bit...and have me right here. The swollen lips between Ella's legs were so wet and throbbing, she could think of nothing else. She desperately wanted him to fill her empty, hollow ache. And impale her with his magnificent sword.

The song ended, and as several couples left the dance floor, Jean-Luc raised Ella to a stand, swirled her to face him, and wrapped his corded arms around the small of her waist. His breath heaving, his deep voice was gruff and hoarse. "Come home with me, Ella. I want to worship every exquisite inch of your divine dancer's body."

Ella had had one night stands before. The promise of passion quickly spent. The embarrassing awkwardness. The inevitable abandonment.

No one had ever asked to *worship every exquisite inch of her divine dancer's body* before. And Ella longed for Jean-Luc with every fiber of her being.

She raised her eyes to his, the intoxicating allure of desire dancing in the dark, smoldering depths. Swallowing his bottom lip into hers, she traced the silky inner lining with the tip of her tongue and whispered fervently into his open mouth, "Yes."

He escorted her back to their table so she could grab her purse and the paper bag containing her charcoal portrait and small painting. Then, the promise of untold pleasures etched across his stubbled, handsome face, Jean-Luc led Ella from the pulsating heat of the *boîte de nuit.*

Into the intoxicating starry night.
Hand in hand, down the cobblestone streets.
Back to the *Atelier des Lumières.*

Chapter 2

A Night to Remember

Jean-Luc unlocked the dark blue wooden door, turned on the light, and led her into his shop. He closed and locked the door behind them, adjusted the blinds, and gently took the purse and parcel from her hand to place on the table. Returning to stand in front of her, he lifted her trembling hand to his warm, full lips. His moustache was soft against her skin. "You are exquisite. And I want you desperately."

Ella searched his fierce, feral face. Lust blazed in his dark eyes. But she saw patience and restraint as well. He was a skilled lover. And he wanted her. She stroked the beard along his chin and whispered, "And I have never wanted any man as much as I want you."

He swept a lock of long hair from her face, leaning down to brush tender lips against hers. He drew her bottom lip into his, his warm mouth igniting the heat between her trembling thighs. His tongue traced the outline of her lips, parting them as he deepened the kiss, tasting, probing, and exploring. He delved deep, claiming every recess of her mouth, wrapping strong arms around her, pulling her body possessively against his.

Eager lips trailed down her throat as he eased the strap of her tank over her shoulder to bare a breast. Ella gasped when his warm, wet mouth latched onto her nipple, sucking intently, drawing the extended tip down his throat. Jean-Luc removed her tank, dropped it on the floor, and lavished both nipples with soft, silken lips. She moaned with pleasure as his hand roamed under her skirt, caressing and stroking the curved back of her bare inner thigh.

He lifted a rough, haggard face. "Let's go upstairs. I want to lay you down on my bed and taste every inch of you."

Ella quivered at the thought. She'd never had a man go down on her before. With a seductive smile, he took her hand and led her up the wooden stairs.

Centered under a large, arched window was a huge bed with a tufted black comforter and several fluffy pillows. Stars winked in the night sky through the curved glass, bathing the dark room in silver starlight. On one side of the spacious studio, a black leather couch and two matching chairs were grouped around a coffee table, and at the other end of the apartment, two black stools stood at a bar along the galley kitchen.

Jean-Luc led her to the bed, and as he turned to face her, he removed the sculpted black t-shirt which accentuated his athletic form.

Ella's breath hitched at the sight of rippled, tattooed torso liberally dusted with dark hair, a long trail leading from the thick expanse across his broad chest, down his muscled abdomen, to disappear into the waist of the torn, tight jeans molded to his sinewy thighs. Her eyes lingered on the burgeoning bulge of his arousal, which he adjusted before opening his arms to welcome her in.

Topless, her long hair cascading down to her waist, she slid into his embrace. His corded, tattooed arms encircled her, his chest hair tickling her erect nipples. "You are exquisite," he whispered, kissing her neck, lowering his lips to suckle each nipple, as he unzipped her denim skirt and slid it to the floor.

Ella was glad she'd worn her pretty black lace underwear, for he admired the curve of her slender hips, running his hands appreciatively over them as he peeled her panties down her trembling thighs.

He sat down on the edge of the bed, his hands on her hips, pulling her toward him to trace her navel with the tip of his tongue. He lowered his face to the thin band of neatly trimmed pubic hair, rubbing his nose along her bikini line, audibly inhaling her scent with a deep, rumbling growl. "God, I want to taste you. Your scent is driving me wild."

With expert fingers, he separated the moist lips between her quivering thighs, lapping and exploring with his tongue and warm mouth. The sensation was unlike anything Ella had ever experienced, and she moaned as he rubbed the tip of his nose and the flat of his tongue against her sensitive bud.

"Mmm," he hummed, the reverberations rippling into her very core, "…delicious. Salty and sweet." He pulled her down onto the bed beside him, laying her upon her back, spreading her legs wide as he knelt on the floor between them. "Open for me, Ella. Let me taste you deep inside."

His skilled lips sucked and slurped, as if she were a delicious dessert. His tongue delved deep into her core, the warm, wet length penetrating and retracting in a rhythmic pulse. He licked his fingers, slipping two, then three, deep inside, pumping steadily as Ella's thighs tightened with increasing tension. He returned his wicked mouth to her throbbing clit, rubbing his tongue and the tip of his nose over her aroused bud in an insistent rhythm with the pounding thrust of his fingers. *Oh, my God, I'm going to come,* Ella realized, as her body clenched onto his fingers, the indescribably delicious waves of pleasure crashing over her like pounding surf as she contracted and convulsed under his nimble tongue.

Replete with pleasure, Ella lay on her back and gazed up at Jean-Luc as he removed his tight, faded jeans. Released from confinement, his erect penis bobbed at attention before her, a droplet near the opening at the tip glistening in the starlight. He slid on a condom and positioned himself between her weakened legs. Nudging her thighs apart with powerful knees, he rubbed the head of his engorged cock along the slick outer folds of her moist, tender flesh.

Probing for the entrance he sought, he slipped the wide head just inside her body, teasing as he withdrew the thick tip, hovering it at her slick opening, making her desperate with want. Again, he allowed just the head to enter her, removing it to rub the hard, slippery ridge against her sensitive clit.

"Please, Jean-Luc, I want you… inside me." Ella wrapped her arms around his muscled back, gripped her legs around his waist, and pulled him down toward her throbbing body, yearning for him to fill the empty, hollow ache.

He slid his hands under her hips, tilted her pelvis up, and with a guttural groan, plunged in deep. With each rhythmic stroke, the wide head of his cock hit just the right spot against her inner wall, the mounting tension bringing Ella to the edge of ecstasy once again.

She gripped him with her thighs, lifting her hips to meet his pounding thrusts, sucking his shoulder and savoring the fresh salty taste of his sweat on her tongue. The tension in his taught muscles increased with each pump of his pulsing hips, until Jean-Luc finally drove to the hilt, convulsing with pleasure as Ella's body clamped his. Clenching him tight in the throes of climax, the rhythmic contractions of her release squeezed him, pumping him dry. She envisioned the hot spurts of fiery, liquid flame pouring from his magnificent body. Filling her inner core.

Limbs entwined, bodies sated, he lingered inside her for a while, then carefully withdrew and removed the condom. Tossing it in the trashcan on the floor beside the bed, he reclined at her side and pulled her into his arms. He kissed her sex-tousled hair and whispered, "That was incredible."

Ella snuggled against his hairy chest, burrowing her nose into the soft, dark curls, savoring his musky, masculine scent. No man had ever gone down on her before. No lover had ever made her come. She'd never experienced a shared orgasm. And, though she knew that a man as handsome and alluring as Jean-Luc could have any woman he wanted—and that this was undoubtedly a one-night stand—Ella was grateful that she'd had this memorable experience.

For Jean-Luc had given her a night to remember that she would treasure for the rest of her life.

"I'll walk you home if you want to go. But I would much prefer it if you'd stay here and sleep in my arms." He kissed the side of her forehead and hugged her tight. "I want to make love to you again in the soft morning light. And have coffee and croissants together." He raised himself onto one arm and leaned down to kiss her softly. "Will you stay with me, *ma belle?* And let me love you as we awake in each other's arms?"

Ella had experienced a few one-night stands. Four before she married Paul. Three since the divorce. Not one had ever considered her pleasure first before his own. Not one had ever asked her to sleep in his arms. And not one had ever wanted to *make love in the soft morning light.*

Her body was sated. But so was her soul. For the first time since Ella could remember, she felt attractive. Desirable. Even... cherished.

With joy that burst forth like a pure, freshwater spring, Ella whispered. "I want to stay... and sleep in your arms."

He flashed her a contented grin and snuggled her against his warm chest. With his generous heart pounding under her ear, and his muscles twitching as he drifted off to sleep, Ella gazed out the window above the bed into the velvety night sky.

And wished upon a star that this unforgettable night would never end.

Chapter 3

Atelier des Lumières

Rays of golden sunlight glimmered in her long blonde hair, luxuriously draped across his rumpled black sheets. One of her willowy arms curled up onto the pillow, exposing a pert breast and soft pink nipple. Her rosy lips were parted in sleep, the delicate bone structure of her elegant face enhanced by her long, slender neck. Jean-Luc marveled at the intriguing beauty in his bed. An intoxicating blend of complex contrasts.

The toned, sculpted muscles and long, lithe limbs of a dancer. The shy exterior, concealing a fiery passion that stirred his body and soul. And, beneath the mirrored surface which masked her pain, a fragile heart which he suspected had been shattered like glass.

He wanted to make love to her, to give her the pleasure she deserved yet inconceivably, had never known. To make her bloom like a neglected rose, nurtured at long last.

With tender fingertips, he stroked a soft breast, tweaking and twirling the nipple, while tracing his tongue in languid circles around the pretty pink peak of the other. She lay on her side in front of him, allowing Jean-Luc access to both breasts while his hardened body rubbed against her soft skin.

Her eyelashes fluttered open, and she hummed as he

suckled one nipple and tweaked the other, lowering his hand to stroke the soft curls between her creamy thighs.

She opened her legs for him, and he probed with a nimble finger, spreading the wet warmth inside all over her aroused little bud. As his finger stroked her clit, he positioned himself to poke and prod from behind, her entrance slippery and slick. He reached for a condom in the drawer of his bedside table, slipped it on.

And plunged into paradise.

Her nubile body gripped him like a vice, clamping on tight as he pumped from behind and pulsed from the front. The upward thrusts of his pelvis matched the downward strokes of his fingers, her delicious body clenching as he drove her closer to the edge.

When she shattered in his arms, the rhythmic contractions of her climax squeezed, pumped, and sucked him dry. His entire body shuddered, the volcanic pulsations explosive as he erupted profusely inside her.

Limbs quivering as he held her, he brushed tender lips against the side of her face. "Mmm," he hummed as he caressed her breast. "The perfect way to start the morning." He withdrew carefully from her body and dropped the condom into the trash. He pushed her tresses away so he could suckle her neck. "You are exquisite, *mon coeur*. A rare, delicate beauty that I just can't get enough of." He swallowed a pink nipple, reveling in her moan of delight.

"I need to use the bathroom," she whispered as she sat up in bed, her long hair spilling down over a shoulder. The tiny pink tip of her nipple peeked through the silky golden sheet, and Jean-Luc couldn't resist touching it.

She arose from the bed with a smile and nodded in the direction of the kitchen. "Is it over there?"

He sprawled languidly across the mattress, his satisfied body awash in a pleasant afterglow. "*Oui*, in the corner, beside the kitchen." He stretched his back, smiling at the curve of her swaying hips as she softly plodded across the bare wooden floor. "I'll make us some coffee."

Ella emerged a few minutes later, dressed in last night's mauve tank top and denim skirt, her glossy blonde hair finger combed, the smudged mascara wiped from her sleepy eyes. Pulling up a barstool, she leaned over the black kitchen countertop to inhale the rich aroma of the steaming coffee as he placed *un bol de café* in front of her.

Between the two breakfast place settings, Jean-Luc set a platter with four flaky croissants, *un pot de confiture,* a jar of honey, and a small tub of butter.

Settling down onto the barstool at her side, he picked up the platter to offer her the typical French breakfast. She smiled and selected a croissant, spread it with butter and raspberry jam, and licked her fingers with childish delight.

Jean-Luc grinned as he sunk his teeth into his own croissant. Wiping his mouth on a napkin, he said, "Although I'd much rather spend the day in bed with you, I do have three art lessons this morning, so I'll walk you home when we've finished breakfast."

A glimmer of disappointment flashed in her deep green eyes.

"But remember...I want to paint you. Would it be alright if I came to fetch you after my lessons are done? Say, around noon? We can get sandwiches to go. I know a quiet park near *le Sacré-Coeur* where we can sit on a bench under the shade trees and have a *pique-nique.*

When we're done, we can come back here, and I'll show you some of my art. And the studio where I'd like to paint you." He took a big gulp of coffee and flashed her his most disarming grin. "Nude, of course."

Her eyes widened as she swallowed a bite of croissant. "Nude?"

"*Mais, oui.* I want to portray your inner fire. The passion I saw and felt last night." His appreciative fingers caressed her cheek. "The sizzling flames beneath the fragile surface. Romantic antithesis. A compelling contrast."

She smiled hesitantly, uncertain eyes searching his face. "I do love the charcoal portrait you sketched of me last night. I'm sure the painting will be incredible, too. But I'm nervous about being painted nude." She traced a finger around the rim of the *bol de café* as she gazed into her coffee.

"Don't be nervous with me, Ella. I want to capture your exquisite beauty on canvas. To make love to you with my art, as well as my body." He lifted her hand to his lips. "I am glad we'll have the whole month of June together." *If I don't scare you away, like the others…*

They finished up, left the *atelier*, and walked along the quiet, quaint streets of Montmartre, just beginning to stir in the early morning light. When they stopped in front of her *résidence* near *la Maison Rose,* Jean-Luc suggested, "Let's exchange phone numbers. You can text or call me if there's any change in plans."

Their contact information shared and stored, he wrapped his arms around Ella's waist and pulled her close. Brushing his lips softly against hers, Jean-Luc promised to return at noon. "*À bientôt, ma belle.* See you soon."

He waited on the street corner until she disappeared into the building, then strode briskly across the cobbled stone square under the clear morning sky. He inhaled Ella's scent on his moustache, his body thickening as he remembered how she'd writhed under his tongue. Today, they'd have the whole afternoon together. He envisioned her long legs wrapped around him, the thick, velvety warmth of her welcoming body... and had to stop and adjust his jeans to finish the trek home.

At the apartment, he showered, tidied up, and prepared for the art lessons. Throughout the interminable morning, he found himself repeatedly thinking of Ella, grateful for the painter's apron which not only protected his clothing, but also concealed his embarrassing, obvious arousal.

When the last lesson was finally done, Jean-Luc checked his messages, relieved that Ella had not canceled. He responded to a few important texts, tucked his phone in his back pocket, and headed out into the warm spring sunlight.

A bouquet of mauve pink roses and plump peonies in the adjacent florist shop reminded him of the tank top she'd worn last night. *The same color as her lips. And nipples.* He paid for the flowers, inhaled the fragrant blossoms, and hoped the impromptu gift would please her.

When he arrived at the *résidence,* Ella was waiting for him in the lobby. She waved to him through the large window, her pretty face lit up in a glorious smile.

Her hair was swept up into a loose chignon on top of her head, a few tendrils curling softly against her cheeks in a style which reminded him of *la Belle Époque,* when Impressionists such as Renoir, Monet, and Van

Gogh had flocked to Montmartre. A stretchy black camisole top accentuated her slim torso, and large pink roses tumbled across the black cotton gypsy skirt which cascaded in voluminous tiers to her ankles. Long earrings sparkled in the sunlight, dangling to the top of her tanned, sculpted shoulders. God, she was beautiful. A *belle bohémienne* to rob him of breath and coherent thought.

Like a graceful ballerina captured on canvas by Degas, Ella floated through the door, her eyes widening in surprise as she accepted the proffered bouquet from Jean-Luc's outstretched hands. Burying her nose in the fat pink blooms, she hummed with pleasure and swayed with obvious delight.

"I love them. Thank you so much!" she exclaimed, reveling in the heady floral scent. Dark green eyes glinted like fine emeralds as she gazed up at him with unabashed joy. "Pink roses and peonies are my favorites."

He snapped a picture—he'd use it to paint the portrait of her sensual delight—and pulled her into an affectionate embrace. Gently claiming her lips with his own, his tongue traced the silky lining inside the soft petals of her rosebud mouth. "I'm glad you like them." He smiled down at her, tucked inside his arms, the flowers cradled protectively against her chest. "Ready to get some lunch?"

She nodded and linked her arm through his offered elbow, burying her nose into the fragrant blooms with a murmur of contentment.

Under the clear blue sky and warm late May sun, he led her to a little glass kiosk with a white awning where they ordered *sandwiches à emporter*, ducking into a *pâtisserie* for two *tartelettes aux cerises* for dessert. When they reached the cobbled stone square with the fabulous view of *le Sacré-Coeur* amidst the familiar shade trees, Ella was awestruck by the cascading branches of light lavender flowers lining the quaint, quiet street. She exclaimed in a whisper of wonder, "Look at the wisteria. It's incredible!"

They settled onto an empty park bench, unwrapped the crusty baguette sandwiches, and dug in, savoring the spicy tang of Dijon mustard over the grilled chicken and Brie topped with lettuce, tomato, and hard-boiled egg. Ella devoured her *sandwich au poulet,* openly admiring the fragrant blooms of purple wisteria which enclosed the picturesque park.

Jean-Luc was captivated by her youthful exuberance, her innate joy at the natural beauty which surrounded them. He wanted to know more about her. She was beguiling. Bewitching.

Breathtaking.

"You mentioned that you're a French teacher from Florida," he said between bites of his sandwich, "and you've come to Montmartre to study art?"

She wiped the mayonnaise from the corner of her mouth. "That's right. For the month of June, I'll be taking French language and culture courses each morning with other teachers from around the world. There will be excursions to various *ateliers* in Paris, and we'll visit some of the museums—*le Musée Rodin, le Louvre, le Centre Pompidou*—to bring back knowledge and experiences to share with our students."

She crumpled the paper her sandwich had been wrapped in, tucking it into the empty bag. "I arrived a few days early— to have time to explore Paris a bit before classes begin on Monday. This morning, I met Yelena, a French teacher from Russia who seems really nice. She speaks no English, and I don't know Russian, so we have to communicate exclusively in French, which is perfect for us to practice our language skills." She smiled up at him, the afternoon sunlight sparkling in her expressive eyes. "You speak English exceptionally well. You must have studied it in school. Have you ever been to the United States?"

He finished the last bite of his sandwich, placing the trash into the paper bag on the bench at his side. "Mmm, hmm," he responded, opening the container of pastries and handing her a *tartelette aux cerises*—a single serving custard pie, topped with dark sweet cherries. As she bit into the scrumptious dessert, humming with approval, he told her about his past.

"I lived in New York City for six years—four spent at NYU, where I earned a degree in fine arts. After graduation, I lived in Manhattan with my girlfriend for two years. When we broke up, she moved home to Ohio, and I came back to France."

He chuckled as Ella moaned in appreciation of the delicious *tartelette aux cerises*. "My friend Florent— he's an artist, too— was living in Montmartre at the time, in the same apartment where I live now. He was giving painting lessons, selling a few of his pieces here and there, doing custom portraits in his studio. He invited me to come to Paris and share both the apartment and *atelier* with him. I set up a bedroom in a studio downstairs, and we shared the kitchen and living room. It worked well for a couple years, until his girlfriend Yolaine moved in, and then things became awkward. They got married about a year and a half ago and moved to Strasbourg. I had just been approved to share a spot on *la Place du Tertre* with another portrait artist, so the extra money I earned from that helped me manage the rent on my own. I get by, but it's tough on just one income."

She nodded as she finished the cherry tart, washing it down with a few swigs of bottled Vittel. "It's the same in Florida. Rent is almost impossible to afford on your own. I have a small one-bedroom apartment, and I barely make ends meet. When I got divorced—I was married for five years—I moved back home with my parents for a few months. I got hired to teach French in a new district, found an apartment, and I've been living there for the past year. But... I don't know what the future holds. I have what they call an annual contract, and I won't know until late July or early August if I even have a job next year. It's really tough for someone who's new to the county. All the best positions are held by teachers with tenure."

He tore a few morsels of bread from the uneaten crust of his sandwich and tossed them at several pigeons pecking crumbs on the cobbled stone square. Brushing his hands on his jeans, he leaned back, crossed his long legs, and extended his arm along the bench behind Ella. The sun was warm on his face as he caressed the soft skin at the back of her neck.

She pulled the phone out of her drawstring purse and leaned against him to take a selfie. "I want to always remember this glorious summer in Montmartre— with the handsome artist who sketched my portrait. And made me feel alive again." She snapped the shot, kissed his lips, and tucked her phone back into her black silky bag. Lifting the bouquet of pink peonies and roses to her nose, she inhaled and savored the heady floral scent. "Thank you again for these gorgeous flowers. I love them."

They lingered on the bench a while longer, enjoying the fragrant wisteria, the lush shade trees, and the ambiance of the quiet park. Jean-Luc traced the supple skin of Ella's shoulder, gliding his fingers down her long, slender arm. He leaned forward to brush his lips along the side of her neck. "I love your hair like this," he whispered into the shell of her delicate ear. "It's the style of *la Belle Époque*, when the Impressionists painted here. Elegant and classy, but with these loose tendrils…" he said, twirling a blonde strand tumbling from her loose *pompadour* around his calloused finger, "…it's bohemian and chic." He sucked the soft skin of her shoulder, trailing his tongue along her throat. "You're exquisite, Ella. A beauty to inspire my art. You're my Muse. *Ma belle bohémienne.*"

He curved a finger under her chin and gently turned her face toward his. Swallowing her soft pink lips with his own, he groaned when she slipped her tongue into his mouth and curved an arm around his neck, pulling him closer. As she melted into him, his body stiffened at the thought of the moist lips between her thighs, so like her alluring, inviting mouth. "Let's go back to the apartment," he said huskily, rising to his feet and adjusting his clothing with a sly grin. *God, I want to bury myself into her.* He took her hand, kissed it, and raised her to a stand. "We have all afternoon…"

Ella's eyes blazed like fiery emeralds. She grabbed her purse and the bouquet of flowers while Jean-Luc tossed their trash into a nearby receptacle. Then, hand in hand, he led her through the fragrant wisteria. Along the cobbled stone streets. Back to the *Atelier des Lumières.*

****

Jean-Luc opened the blue wooden door, escorted Ella into his workshop, and locked the entrance behind him. He lowered the blinds and placed the *Fermé* sign on the window so that they would not be disturbed.

Ella was admiring some of the paintings on the wall, but his body throbbed with longing as his eyes roved over her silken skin and the alluring curve of her hips. Walking up behind her, he wrapped his arms around her waist, coaxing both of her nipples into stiff peaks with strokes of his thumbs. He pressed his hardened length into her rounded butt, aching to plunge into her welcoming warmth. He did want to show her his art, but he needed to relieve the painful ache in his loins first. There would be plenty of time for art appreciation after he worshipped her beautiful body.

And emptied himself into her.

She leaned back against him, rubbing her soft rump on the iron rod in his tight jeans, lifting her pert little nipples to receive the firm caresses of his fingers.

He traced his tongue along the side of her neck, cupping and stroking her breasts as he ground himself into her backside. He glanced at the nearby table and imagined laying her over it, lifting her skirt, and plunging into her right here. But the condoms were in the drawer of his bedside table.

"Let's go upstairs. I need you *now*." Jean-Luc stepped back away from her delicious body, took her hand, and led her up to the bedroom.

The afternoon sun streamed through the high arched window, gilding the sumptuous bed in golden light. Jean-Luc turned Ella to face him, sliding her camisole top up over her shoulders. He lowered his lips to suckle the irresistible pink peaks that poked at his face, clamoring for oral adoration.

He rolled alternate nipples between his lips, tugging, lapping, and sucking as Ella moaned and swooned. Jean-Luc pulled her long gypsy skirt down over her hips, then tugged her black lace panties to her ankles, helping her to step out of her clothes and recline on the edge of the bed.

Kneeling between her trembling thighs, he greedily pushed her legs apart, exposing the glistening tender pink flesh. "*Mon Dieu*, you are beautiful…" he groaned, spreading her luscious lips open, probing the wetness inside, and sucking the succulent cream off his gleaming fingers. "And you taste delicious."

He plunged three fingers deep inside, lowering his hungry mouth to her warm, wet folds. With slow, rhythmic thrusts, he penetrated her soft flesh, worshipping her engorged clit with reverent lips as she writhed and moaned under his skilled tongue.

As Jean-Luc sensed the tension mounting in her thighs and lower stomach, Ella tipped her pelvis up to meet his pulsing hand, her plush warmth tightly clenching his long fingers. He increased the pace of his thrusts, inundating her sensitive little bud with a hard, insistent tongue. He pumped her mercilessly until she convulsed in spasms, clamping and contracting on his fingers.

Breathless, her legs splayed wide, she lay under him, enticingly open and impossibly irresistible. He jumped to his feet, peeled off his jeans and t-shirt, his erection throbbing as it bobbed in the air. Reaching into the drawer of the nightstand, he grabbed a condom, slipped it on, and knelt on the bed between Ella's quivering legs.

He leaned down to suckle her breasts, nudged her

thighs apart, and slipped his hands under her receptive hips. Tilting her pelvis up, he rubbed the hard ridge of his cock along her slick flesh, probing the entrance and spreading her wetness over his thick, swollen head.

She wrapped her legs around his waist, pulling him toward her. "I want you inside me...please," she whimpered, emitting a guttural moan as he plunged in deep. Ella's arms folded around his shoulders and her ankles enlaced his hips, drawing him deeper inside as she rose up to meet his fierce, urgent thrusts.

Her slick, tight grip squeezed him like a delicious vice. He pounded her relentlessly, his engorged flesh ready to burst as the fiery liquid within rose with increasing pressure and throbbing tension. When the delicious fountain spewed forth at last, he thrust in deep, shuddering as waves of ecstasy flowed from him in exquisite, profound relief.

Savoring a few moments of physical bliss, he shifted his weight onto one elbow so as to not crush her. He grinned down at Ella and exhaled, "You drive me wild." Her full lips beckoned, so he plundered them softly with his own before rolling onto his back to discreetly dispose of the condom.

Ella moved onto her side and nestled her head under his shoulder, burying her nose in his chest hair. "Mmm," she murmured, "I love your scent. It stirs something deep inside me." She lay contentedly in his arms, stroking the dark hair and kissing his skin where a tattoo curled up the left side of his abdomen. "A flamenco dancer," she whispered appreciatively. "As gorgeous as the one in the painting I bought— *La Alma*." Tracing her fingers along the dancer's curved, elegant arms, she asked hesitantly, "Was she your lover?"

Jean-Luc pulled Ella against his chest, rocking her gently as he kissed the top of her head. "No… she was a dancer I admired. Her name was Carmen. She was the star of the flamenco troupe that my parents belonged to—*Flamenco del Sol*." He stroked the side of her soft cheek and smiled at her inquisitive face. "I used to watch Carmen dance when I was a boy learning flamenco in my parents' troupe. I did have a huge crush on her, but we were never lovers. She was much older—my parents' age. But she was my idol. As well as the inspiration for my own dance."

A glint of surprise sparked in her emerald eyes.

He tucked an arm under his head and met her rapt gaze. "I'm a flamenco dancer, like my parents." He grinned as her eyes widened in wonder. "My father, Jose Cortés, was a flamenco dancer from Spain. He met my mother, Solange Dubois—a French artist from Provence who was also a dancer— in Córdoba. They fell in love and joined the *Flamenco del Sol* dance troupe, performing together across Spain and France, all the way from Andalucía to *la Côte d' Azur*." He pushed a strand of hair from Ella's enthralled face. "They divorced when I was sixteen, and my mother moved to Perpignan—in the south of France, on the Mediterranean. I learned art from my French mother, and flamenco from my Spanish father. He died when I was eighteen, and the trust fund he'd set up enabled me to go to New York to study art. In Manhattan, I earned extra money performing in flamenco shows. And now, in Montmartre, I dance at the *Tablao Flamenco*—the same place I took you last night. Twice a week, on Tuesday and Friday nights."

Ella sat up and inhaled sharply, her eyes aflame. "Today is Friday. So…you perform tonight?"

He arose from the bed and stretched his arms overhead. "I do indeed. The show starts at eight." He took Ella's hands and pulled her to a stand, enveloping her in his welcoming arms. "I'd like you to come to the performance tonight. Bring your friend Yelena, too. I want you to watch me dance. Because tonight, Ella, *I dance for you*." He lifted her chin gently with a curved finger, leaning down to swallow her full, luscious lips.

"I would love to see you dance!" she whispered breathlessly, burying her face in his chest hair. She looked up at him with incredulous eyes. "And you're going to dance *for me*?"

"Oui, mon coeur. Tonight, I dance for you." He pulled her close, caressing her face with tenderness, as he planted a soft kiss on her parted lips. With an impish grin, he gazed down at her, wrapped up in his arms. "Would you like to see some of my art? Now that we've made love, I can think clearly again." He chuckled deeply as he kissed the corner of Ella's smiling lips.

Her eyes danced with childish delight. "I'd love that!"

Jean-Luc took Ella's hand and led her downstairs. It was exhilarating to share his works with her, all the more exciting because they were both still nude.

Spotting the bouquet of roses and peonies on the table near the entrance door, Ella asked, "I'd like to put these in water. Do you have a vase?"

"I think there's one here, from when Yolaine lived with Florent. She used to buy flowers all the time for the apartment." He looked in a cupboard under the sink where he cleaned his paintbrushes. "Ah…here's one." He handed it to Ella, who arranged the flowers in the clear glass container.

She filled it with water and placed it on the table, beaming with satisfaction as she bent to breathe in the floral fragrance. "There, now they'll last for a few days. Thank you again, Jean-Luc. I just love them."

He grinned, enormously pleased that she liked his gift.

Ella strode across the room to admire the paintings on the wall. "These are beautiful!" she whispered in awe. "They're all flamenco dancers. And each one is magnificent."

He walked up behind her, overlapping his arms across her waist as he kissed the side of her face. "Like Degas, I love to portray dancers. But, while he painted ballerinas, I prefer flamenco." He squeezed Ella tight and nibbled on her ear. "Pure passion."

She kissed his forearms, then wriggled free to examine his works more closely. "You've captured the elegance and grace of movement. The power and precision of form. And the intensity of emotion on their faces." She swirled toward him, her emerald eyes ablaze. "Your work is incredible. I'm amazed by your astounding talent."

Jean-Luc smiled as he beheld the nude temptress before him. Her upswept blonde hair— half tumbling down from their romantic interlude—the lithe limbs, toned body… He just couldn't get enough of her. And yet, she was unaware of her own beauty, her allure, her effect on him. His eyes rove over her lightly tanned skin, admiring the slender torso, narrow waist, and curved hips. When his appreciative gaze settled on the white outline of her bikini and the trimmed hair between her sculpted thighs, his body thickened with a sudden jolt of desire. He'd never been so attracted to a woman before.

God, he wanted her again.

But he also wanted to capture her inner fire on canvas.

Instead of leading her back to bed, which his aroused body urged him to do, he extended his hand. "Come, let me show you the studio where I want to paint your portrait."

He led Ella into a spacious *atelier* with ivory plastered walls and potted plants where a black velvet sofa was situated in the center of the room. Lush, dense foliage concealing an outdoor stone privacy wall was visible through the enormous, sunlit window which extended from the high ceiling to the gleaming pinewood floor. In the corner of the tranquil chamber, a large studio lamp emitted soft, diffused light.

"I'll have you recline on this sofa." He indicated the luxurious, tufted divan. "The natural light from the window will be perfect."

Ella ran appreciative fingers over the soft, decadent fabric. She looked up at him with uncertain eyes.

"Lie down on your right side, facing me. And bend one arm up behind your head."

She positioned herself on the couch, attempting to rearrange her falling hair.

"Take it down, and let it cascade over your shoulder." Jean-Luc adjusted the studio light as she unwound her tumbling tresses. "Here, I'll take those." He accepted the pins she'd removed from her *pompadour* and placed them on a small table beside the easel he'd set up. "Lay back, open your thighs just a bit...yes, like that. Now, look at me...and think of what I just did to you upstairs. Imagine my tongue between your legs, my fingers thrusting deep inside you."

She parted her lips and exhaled as a decadent flush swept across her beautiful face.

Jean-Luc leaned over her, placing a few strands of long blonde hair strategically over her left breast. The pretty pink nipple protruded from the golden cascade, and his lips ached to suckle it. With difficulty, he resisted, returning instead to sketch her outline on the canvas at his easel. "Lift your chin slightly," he instructed. "And imagine what I'm going to do to you tonight after the performance."

Desire blazed in her dark green eyes as a soft moan escaped her parted lips. His body stirred at the sensual sound, her velvety voice strumming him like a harp. Long golden legs, enticingly open—but just a bit—tempted him to push them apart and reveal the glistening pink flesh which clenched him so tight.

His fingers etched her slender curves onto the canvas. "You are exquisite, Ella. I'm attracted to you more than any woman ever before." The pencil danced as the outline of her alluring body emerged under his skilled fingers. "I can't believe how much I want you… I think about you constantly." He captured her pert little breasts, longing to caress the creamy skin. "I haven't been in a relationship for months. But now…I want you with me all the time. I just can't get enough of you." As he sketched the soft curls between her lithe thighs, his cock thickened and lengthened until he stood high and hard, aching for her again. "Ella, I can't resist you," he groaned, tossing his pencil aside and striding briskly to the sofa. He tugged her legs toward him, pulling her so that she lay flat on her back. Hovering over her, he lowered his appreciative mouth to her soft breasts, assailing her luscious nipples with warm, insistent lips.

Ella ran her fingers through his long, thick hair, stroking the back of his head and moaning with pleasure as he traced his tongue along one nipple and twirled the other between his fingertips. She opened her legs for him as he trailed his lips down her abdomen, concentrating his oral adoration on her aroused bud.

With trembling fingers, he stroked and probed her wet warmth, his cock throbbing with need. "*Merde*," he spat, "the condoms are upstairs."

Ella reached for him, grasping his shoulders to keep him close. "You haven't been with a woman in months. And I haven't been with a man either. I'm on the pill, so there's no risk of pregnancy." He drowned in the depths of her limpid eyes. "I want all of you, Jean-Luc. I want to feel you come inside me." She slid her body underneath his, pulling him over her as he lowered himself between her thighs. She reached down to stroke him, smearing the liquid at the tip of his penis with her thumb as she guided him to the entrance of her open, inviting core.

Her moist flesh yielded as he slipped his sensitive head inside, withdrawing it slowly, bobbing in and out. Without the condom, the sensation was incredible. Indescribable. Irresistible.

Ella wrapped her legs around him and lifted herself up, trying to pull him in.

Unable to hold back, he plunged in deep, groaning with almost unbearable pleasure. Her warm, lush flesh clenched his shaft and enveloped his sensitive head in a slick, tight grip. He pounded into her, his balls slapping against the curve of her butt, the thick head of his cock ramming her to the hilt.

Legs flexing around his waist, she matched his

fervent thrusts, sheathing him in molten fire. Her velvety core clamped around him like a tightening vice, increasing the tension until at last she shattered, the spasms of her climax squeezing him in rhythmic contractions. He erupted in powerful, pulsating jets, filling her dark depths with liquid flame.

Supporting his weight on bent forearms, he lowered his head to rest upon her shoulder, moaning softly as she stroked his long hair. "Without a condom, the sensation is incredible. I can't believe how good it felt." He raised his face to kiss her rosebud mouth. "You are exquisite, my beautiful Ella." He pushed himself to a stand, gazing appreciatively at her reclined form as she stretched languidly and hummed in contentment.

He glanced at the clock on the wall. "I have to be at the *tablao* at five. Let's get dressed, and I'll walk you home. When you come to the show tonight, tell the hostess Élodie that you're my guest. I'll have her reserve a table for you and Yelena in the center front of the stage." He helped Ella to a stand and pulled her against his chest. "So I can dance *la soleá* just for you."

They went back upstairs and gathered their hastily discarded clothes. "What time should Yelena and I come tonight?" Ella asked as she wriggled the rose floral gypsy skirt up over her hips.

He watched her pretty pink nipples disappear as she pulled the black camisole over her head and smoothed it down her lean torso. *A dancer's body. The perfect Muse to inspire my art. And satisfy me, body and soul.* He blinked, rousing himself from the pleasant reverie. "They serve dinner before the show, and seating starts at six, so you should be there about quarter till. Tonight, they have a *prix fixe* menu— an appetizer, the main course, a selection of fine wines, and fabulous desserts. Don't worry about the bill—I'll take care of that. You and Yelena are my guests." He pulled on his jeans and zipped up the fly. "The show starts at eight and lasts about an hour. After the performance, stay at your table and enjoy the wine. I'll take a quick shower backstage, get dressed, and come join you. I know a great club where we can dance salsa and merengue. Should I fix Yelena up with a friend so she can come with us, too?"

"I'm not sure. I'll ask her when I get back to the *résidence* and text you." Ella slung her purse over her shoulder and glanced at the bouquet of roses and peonies.

Reading her thoughts, Jean-Luc suggested, "Leave them here. We'll be coming back to the atelier. That is... if you want to spend the night again?" He pulled her into his arms and kissed her softly. Invitingly. "And, if you don't have any plans tomorrow, we can explore Paris a bit." He grinned at her enthusiastic nod of approval. "I work tomorrow night—I do portrait sketches on *la Place du Tertre* at six— but we'll have the whole day together. That is, if you'd like to."

She squealed with delight. "I'd love to! That sounds perfect."

He kissed her hand, led her outside, and locked the *Atelier des Lumières.*

Under a vibrant sky steaked pink and purple by the slanted rays of the setting sun, Jean-Luc escorted his bohemian Muse home.

Chapter 4

La Soleá

Ella trotted up the stairs inside the *résidence* and stopped into her room before going down the hall to talk to Yelena. She strolled past the single bed nestled against the light beige wall and dropped her purse on top of the wooden table in the corner. She opened the blinds to let in the warm sunshine and the window for the fresh spring breeze.

In the compact kitchen, there was a tiny refrigerator, a microwave on the counter, two white cupboards and a sink next to the small stove. She grabbed a bottle of *Évian* from the fridge and went into the bathroom to put her hair up in a topknot.

She finished the bottle of water, left her room, and headed down the corridor to knock on Yelena's door.

Expressive brown eyes and a friendly smile greeted her. "Hi, Ella! Come on in. Did you have a nice lunch with your handsome artist?"

Ella entered the room which mirrored her own. The enticing aroma of freshly brewed coffee beckoned. "Mmm... the coffee smells good."

"I'll pour you a cup. Cream and sugar?"

"Just cream, please." Ella accepted the mug and sat on the edge of the neat bed covered by a dark blue comforter. "Thank you. I need a cup." She took a sip and hummed with pleasure. French coffee was so good!

Although she and Jean-Luc conversed in both French and English, with Yelena, Ella spoke only French. "We had a lovely picnic in a shady park with beautiful wisteria blossoms. It was so nice…" She took another swig of the delicious brew and sighed with contentment. "I discovered something incredible about Jean-Luc. He's not only an artist, but he's also a flamenco dancer! He performs at the *Tablao Flamenco* twice a week, and he has invited both of us to come watch him dance tonight. The show starts at eight, but they serve dinner first. Seating begins at six, so he suggested we arrive about ten minutes early. He said the hostess Élodie will escort us to a reserved table right in front of the stage." Ella leaned forward, breathless with excitement. "Yelena—he said that tonight, he is dancing *for me*. Can you believe it? I can't wait!" Realizing that Yelena hadn't even accepted the invitation, Ella asked, "Are you free tonight? Will you come with me?"

Yelena squeezed Ella's hand. "Of course, I will come with you. I've never seen a flamenco performance before. It will be another fascinating story to tell my students when I return to the classroom."

Ella finished her coffee. "Jean-Luc wants to take me dancing after the show. He offered to fix you up with one of his friends. Would you like to come with us?"

Yelena strolled into the kitchen to rinse out the empty coffee cups. "Thank you for the invitation, but I'm married. And my husband would not appreciate it if I went to a nightclub and danced with another man. No, I'll pass, but thank you any way."

"Well, Jean-Luc and I will walk you home after the show. I am so excited—I can't wait to watch him dance!"

Ella stood and smoothed her gypsy skirt. "It's nearly five, so I'll head back to my room and get ready. I'll come get you about five thirty, ok?"

"Perfect. I'll be ready. Oh, Ella…this is so romantic! A handsome French painter who's a flamenco dancer, too. Sweeping you off your feet with his charisma and charm. What a memorable summer this will be!" Yelena swooned with vicarious delight.

"I know… I still can't believe it." Ella shook her head in disbelief and headed out the door. "See you soon!" With a spring in her step, she practically danced down the hall.

A half hour later, Yelena and Ella strolled gaily down the cobbled stone street to the *Tablao Flamenco* where a smiling Élodie led them into the gilded purple glow of the cave-like hall.

Clad in the traditional white shirt and black pants, an amiable waiter served them a bottle of *Meursault*—the same dry, white burgundy wine that Jean-Luc had selected when he'd brought Ella here the last time. The delectable appetizer was a puff pastry filled with *escalibada*—warm goat cheese and roasted onions, and the *plat principal* was grilled salmon with sweet potato purée. For dessert, an intriguing blend of five chocolate confections completed the sumptuous meal.

As the waiters throughout the *tablao* cleared the tables, musicians and flamenco dancers came onto the stage in preparation for the impending performance. A hush fell across the audience as the guitarists, percussionists, and violinists began to play a slow, romantic melody.

Five female dancers in brightly colored dresses with tiers of cascading ruffles started swaying, their arms circling overhead, their bodies interpreting the emotional theme of the music. As the tempo increased, the thick, pointed black heels of the dancers' shoes frapped frenetically against the wooden stage floor in precise, intricate footwork that punctuated the rhythm of the drums.

When their dance ended, the five flamenco performers retreated to the back of the theater amid tremendous applause as Jean-Luc made his entrance upon the stage.

Brilliant purple beams focused on him in the spotlight, while the musicians and other dancers lingered in darkened shadows.

He was dressed entirely in black, his long dark hair cascading loosely over his shoulders, hanging down his expansive back. Form-fitting pants clung to his long legs, emphasizing the bulging muscles in his powerful thighs. An open jacket with long tuxedo tails revealed his bare, sculpted torso and rippled abdomen, where the familiar tattoo of the flamenco dancer twirled sensuously up his left side.

Ella's breath hitched as she beheld him. He was magnificent. Intoxicating. Mesmerizing.

As three guitarists began playing, the purple lights illuminated them, and Jean-Luc moved in rhythm with the slow, plaintive melody. He extended his arms and raised them high overhead, lifting the sides of his jacket like windswept wings of an eagle about to take flight. Undulating his hips as his arms joined together over his head, he lifted an impassioned face to the sky, the melancholy notes of the music evoking the suffering of his soul.

He clenched a fist high above his upturned face,

pulling his hand down slowly, opening his fingers to trace his forehead, bearded chin, and elongated, exposed neck. He stopped the descent of his hand from the sky to form a fist clenched protectively over his vulnerable heart. Wrapping the sides of his jacket to envelop his torso, like a wounded hawk tucking its wings, Jean-Luc raised an anguished face to the crowd.

And penetrated Ella with piercing, impassioned eyes.

The music increased in tempo, the flamenco dancers in the background clapping in rhythm with the drums, as Jean-Luc slammed the heels of his pointed black boots against the wooden stage, his body as much of a percussion instrument as the *cajón* itself. Swirling around the stage, he lifted the sides of his jacket like a swooping swan, bending at the waist and flinging his hair back as he lifted his torso, his feet matching the frenetic rhythm of the beat.

Building in crescendo, the staccato of the violins amplified Jean-Luc's intense, intricate footwork while the woeful wails of the singer cried out in pain. Faster and faster, his feet frapped against the stage as he approached Ella, the intensity building like an impending climax. He removed his jacket, his tattooed skin glistening under the bright lights, and flung it provocatively at her.

Ella caught it, clutching the jacket against her breast, barely able to breathe.

Half-naked, feet flying, legs pounding the wooden floor, Jean-Luc danced magnificently before her.

Beckoning. Beguiling. Bewitching.

With his gleaming skin, piercing eyes, and heaving breath, it was as if he were making love to her, his impassioned gaze penetrating her very soul.

In the throes of climax, he spun in tight, dizzying circles, arms outstretched at his sides, feet slamming against the stage. When the music ended, he halted abruptly in front of her, the sudden silence a profound, amplifying effect.

Bowing to her like a chivalrous knight before his beloved queen, Jean-Luc lifted his powerful, bent torso. Flicked his hair to slap against his broad, bare back. And flung droplets in a spray of sweat across Ella's enthralled face.

As if—in his sensuous, passionate dance—he had come all over her.

Breathless, Ella's pulse pounded furiously, mesmerized by his fierce, feral gaze.

Dark, seductive eyes held her fast as intense heat spread like wildfire throughout Ella's body, molten liquid pooling between her trembling thighs.

Smoldering, sizzling, and scorching, the flames of flamenco ignited her inner core.

While Ella sat, stunned and stupefied by Jean-Luc's devastating dance, the final flamenco performance—a festive *bulería*—concluded the evening event.

After erupting in raucous cheers and wildly enthusiastic applause, the appreciative audience began filtering out of the cave-like *tablao,* their smiling faces indicating their obvious enjoyment of the evening.

While they waited for Jean-Luc to change in the backstage dressing room, Yelena leaned across the table to hug Ella in breathless delight. "That was fantastic! I have never seen a flamenco performance before. It was incredible. And Jean-Luc's dance? Oh, Ella…it was magnificent! So personal… so intimate." She squeezed

Ella's hand, her eyes shining with awe. "You'll remember this unforgettable night for the rest of your life."

Ella downed the rest of her wine and spotted Jean-Luc heading toward the table. He'd changed into a black t-shirt and faded jeans, and his damp hair was combed away from his bearded face, tumbling over his shoulders and down his back. With agile grace and simmering strength, he strode purposefully across the *tablao*, his dark eyes fixed upon Ella.

Her breath hitched in anticipation as he swooped down to lift her off the chair and into his arms. His warm, full lips swallowed hers, his corded arms wrapping around her back, pulling her into a full-body embrace that made her swoon. Nuzzling her neck, he finally came up for air, dark eyes dancing with desire as he whispered, "I danced just for you, *mon coeur*."

"It was magnificent. I was mesmerized. Enthralled." She burrowed her nose into the tuft of dark hair at the base of his throat, savoring the distinctly male scent, inhaling it deep into her lungs.

Jean-Luc chuckled deeply, then stepped away to greet Yelena, who was smiling discreetly, trying to avert her eyes. "You must be Yelena," he said jovially, raising her hand to his lips for a gallant, welcoming kiss. "*Enchanté*."

Yelena couldn't contain her exuberance. "You are a fabulous dancer, Jean-Luc! I've never seen a flamenco performance before. It was astounding! I am in absolute awe of your amazing talent. Thank you for inviting me."

"My pleasure," he grinned, hugging Ella with one arm wrapped around her shoulders as he nodded humbly to Yelena. "Are you sure you won't join us? I'm taking

Ella to a club where we can dance salsa and merengue. Wouldn't you like to come, too?"

Yelena smiled ruefully and shook her head. "Thank you, but no. My husband wouldn't like me dancing with another man. If you don't mind, I'd prefer to just return to *la résidence.*"

"Of course. Ella and I will walk you home." Jean-Luc nodded goodbye to several other dancers who were also leaving the *tablao* as he escorted Ella and Yelena through the exit door, out into the starry night sky.

Once they had dropped Yelena off, Jean-Luc grabbed Ella's hand and grinned. "I'm starved. Let's get something to eat before we go to the club. I know a place that has great seafood. Sound good?"

Ella nodded enthusiastically. "Sounds perfect. I love seafood."

Hand in hand, under a twinkling, starlit sky, they strolled along the cobbled stone paths of Montmartre until they arrived at a brasserie with outdoor tables arranged under a canopy of bright red awnings.

Seating her at the table, then taking his place across from her, Jean-Luc ordered a bottle of wine and asked if Ella liked oysters.

"I prefer shrimp or scallops," she replied with a smile. "Since Yelena and I already ate, I'm not very hungry. Maybe just an appetizer?"

"Ok, I'll order oysters for me, shrimp for you, and *langoustines* for us both. They're small lobsters—and the flavor is incredible. You've got to try them."

"You've convinced me. They sound delicious."

The waiter poured two glasses of wine and served Ella six *crevettes* and Jean-Luc a dozen *huîtres*. The platter of *langoustines* would be served when they'd finished the appetizers.

A mischievous glint in his smoldering eyes, he speared the oyster with the small fork, prying it from the shell and raising it to his open lips.

Transfixed, Ella watched as Jean-Luc slid his tongue over the succulent flesh, his gaze never leaving hers. "Salty and sweet. As luscious as the tender lips between your legs." With a soft slurp, he suckled, savored, and swallowed the oyster before her awestruck eyes.

Imagining his skilled tongue on her *tender lips*, Ella's flesh caught fire.

As if he knew the effect it had on her, Jean-Luc slowly sampled another oyster, lifting the shell to his mouth so that he could taste it, twirling his tongue as he licked and lapped the moist flesh, sucking it out of the shell and smacking his lips as he swallowed it. "Mmm," he hummed. "Makes me want to slip under the table and spread your legs wide… and do this to you."

Ella jumped as desire jolted her.

Slowly, deliberately, he lavished his tongue over each oyster, savoring the exquisite flavor as much as the sensuous effect on Ella, who hadn't even touched her food.

Realizing her mouth was agape, she closed her lips on the wineglass and took an awkward gulp. Her mouth was dry, and her legs were quivering.

"Tonight, *mon coeur*. I promise." His seductive smile stirred Ella's soul as the waiter placed the platter of steaming *langoustines* on the table alongside a pot of melted butter. "But first, you must taste this." With the seafood fork, Jean-Luc peeled a portion of the meat from the shell, dipped it in the melted butter, and raised the *langoustine* to her lips. "Open your mouth," he whispered, his eyes alight with promise.

Ella complied, her limbs quavering in his intoxicating presence.

He placed the lobster on her tongue, and she slipped it into her mouth, savoring the delectable flavor of the sweet seafood with the slightly salty, creamy butter. "Now, a swallow of wine. To perfectly enhance the *langoustine.*"

She swirled the *Meursault* on her tongue, savoring the dry, fruity blend against her palate. It was indeed a stellar complement to the delicate flavor of the lobster, and Ella delighted in every bite.

When they finished eating, Jean-Luc paid the bill, stood, and took hold of Ella's hand. As he raised her to a stand, he said with a sly grin, "Now, let's go to the *Loca Luna*. I want to teach you to dance salsa."

Inside the trendy club, a pulsing, thumping beat was both enticing and exhilarating. Jean-Luc led Ella onto the crowded dance floor and pulled her into his arms.

She rested a hand upon his shoulder as he gently gripped her waist, raising her other hand within his just above her shoulder.

"When I step forward with my right foot, you step back with your left." He held her tight, guiding her into his rhythm. "Sway your hips as you move. Yes, just like that."

He taught her the basic pattern of steps, encouragement and pride reflecting in his eyes as she quickly caught on. Soon, Ella was twirling and dipping in his skilled arms, breathless with excitement.

When the tempo changed, Jean-Luc placed his hands on her hips, swaying them rhythmically and provocatively to the pounding, steady beat. He held her tight against his muscled body, causing her to practically swoon in his arms, then spun and swirled her away, snapping her back into his balancing embrace.

She let herself go, trusting his strength and fluid grace, as if she were floating and soaring in his powerful, capable hands. *Like when we make love, and I lose myself in the pleasure he gives...*

Pressing his hardened body against her shimmying hips, he groaned into the shell of her ear. "This is torture. I can't take any more. Let's go back to the apartment."

Ella wanted nothing more. She accepted his outstretched hand. Exited the steamy, sexy *Loca Luna*. And let Jean-Luc lead her back to the *Atelier des Lumières*.

****

Wisps of moonlight filtered through the high arched window onto the sumptuous bed, illuminating it with mystery and magic. A blanket of stars twinkled in the night sky as Jean-Luc drew Ella toward him, swaying in a seductive dance.

"You are irresistible, *mon coeur*." His full lips sought the side of her neck, sucking softly but insistently as he lifted her mauve tank up over her shoulders and tossed it aside.

Her bare breasts tingled in the cool night air, forming perk peaks which ached for his warm, skilled lips. While he suckled and lavished attention on her erect nipples, sending waves of wet warmth between her throbbing thighs, he slid a hand up under her silky skirt to stroke her soft skin.

Ella's legs quivered as deft fingers pushed aside her lace panties and probed her slick, sensitive folds.

"I just can't get enough of you. I want you so much,

it hurts…" An iron hard shaft prodded her stomach as his fingers penetrated her moist flesh.

Remembering his passionate flamenco performance in the *tablao*— how he'd flung beads of sweat upon her, as if he had come for her in his dance—Ella felt emboldened.

She unzipped his jeans, releasing his swollen cock from the confines of his clothing as she sat down on the edge of the bed. Looking up at his impassioned, anguished face, she murmured in a breathy, raspy voice, "I want to watch you come. I want to see it spurt out, like a fountain, all over me. Like tonight, when you splattered me with sweat in your dance."

He moaned as she lapped the hard ridge of his head, sliding the tip of her tongue between the two sensitive halves where a drop of his salty, bitter seed overflowed.

Licking the inside of her palm, she grasped his shaft firmly as she took him into her mouth, sliding his thick girth between her wet, eager lips. With a tight grip of her hand underneath her mouth, she plunged down upon him, lapping and twirling her tongue and lips along the hard ridge of his head, pressing her lips together firmly. With relentless rhythm, she pummeled him, sensing his thigh muscles tighten as his abdomen clenched.

He groaned huskily, "I'm going to come…" and pulled himself from Ella's mouth.

Reclining onto her elbows as he leaned over her, Ella watched in awe as powerful plumes of white, creamy liquid spewed forth all over her breasts. When he'd finished erupting, she sat up and slipped him back into her mouth, sucking the last few drops to savor the taste of him.

He jumped with a jolt of sensation, then gently

withdrew himself from her mouth. Curving a finger under her chin, he lifted her face to look at him as he smiled down upon her. "No woman has ever asked me to do that. God, Ella, you are incredible!"

Humming with contentment, she rubbed the ebullient cream into her breasts. "I'm lathered in Jean-Luc," she purred.

He walked into the adjacent kitchen area and returned with a damp cloth. "Here, use this," he chuckled softly, "so the sheets don't stick to you."

Ella grinned and wiped off her creamy breasts.

Jean-Luc took the cloth, laid it on the marble mantle of the nearby windowsill, then returned his attention to her. He knelt between her legs and pushed her knees apart. Dark eyes dancing in the moonlight, he lowered his lips to her neatly trimmed, soft curls.

Parting her wet folds with his long fingers, he closely examined her glistening flesh. "Provocatively tempting." He lowered his lips to her quivering quim, grinning up at her as he lapped and slurped. "And delightfully *delicious*."

Ella lost herself as his insistent tongue focused on her sensitive bud while three of his long fingers pounded and penetrated her in a perfect, relentless rhythm. Clutching the sides of the bed, she arched and tightened like a tightly drawn arrow, begging for release. Finally, as waves of pleasure crashed over her, she careened over the edge, convulsing and contracting in an explosive climax that left her stomach quaking.

Replete with pleasure, she collapsed back onto the bed as Jean-Luc crawled over her, high and hard once more. "Making you come has made me want you again. Spread your legs for me, Ella. "

He pummeled them both into a shattering, shared climax, then cradled her against his chest with a contented smile. "Tomorrow, I'll show you some of the secrets of Paris. But for now, *mon coeur...* come sleep upon my heart."

He is the most romantic man I have ever known. He makes me feel alive. Alluring. Attractive. I pray he doesn't lose interest, like the others. At least not until the end of June.

Ella sensed his limbs twitching as he drifted off to sleep. Peering through the arched window above the bed where they lay entwined, she spotted a glimmer in the dark night sky. Closing her eyes and holding her breath, she wished once more upon the star that this memorable summer would never end.

Chapter 5

Licked by Flames

The aroma of fresh coffee and delicious food emanated from the adjacent kitchen as Ella stretched and awoke in a contented haze. Morning sunlight streamed in through the high, arched window above the bed, the cloudless blue sky promising a glorious day to discover the secrets of Paris with her handsome, bohemian artist.

She rolled to her side and spotted Jean-Luc in his kitchen, clad only in snug, faded jeans which hugged his tight butt and clung to his muscular thighs. His rippled, tattooed torso was visible over the countertop from her reclining perspective in the bed, and she feasted her eyes on his sculpted physique, reliving the previous night's passion as she observed her half-naked chef create a culinary masterpiece.

His long, black hair was tied in a ponytail which hung down his bare back, and as he set the countertop with turquoise ceramic plates and glasses of freshly squeezed orange juice, he noticed that she was watching him. "Ah, my beauty awakens..." he chuckled deeply, an expansive grin illuminating his handsome face where the trimmed beard outlined his chiseled jawline like a perfectly framed portrait.

Ella slipped from the bed and plodded softly across the pinewood floor to join him in the black and white kitchen. Long blonde hair tumbling over her small breasts and cascading to her waist, she stood nude beside the counter and admired his work.

Beside each teal plate—one of which displayed an incredibly appetizing omelet— he had placed half of a juicy ripe melon, the sweet, fruity fragrance making Ella's mouth water. An enticing array of four pastries was nestled between two large *bols de café,* whose creamy coffee goodness was impossible to resist.

As she sipped her bowl of the rich, robust brew— moaning in delight—Jean-Luc lifted the skillet from the stovetop and flashed her a dazzling grin. "We French usually eat omelets for dinner. But, after six years in the United States, I now prefer them for breakfast." He slid a perfect spinach omelet onto the plate in front of her. "*Une omelette aux épinards,*" he announced proudly, rinsing the pan and placing it into the sink. "Loaded with mushrooms and melted g*ruyère.*"

Ella needed to use the bathroom and wanted to put on some clothes. "You are amazing, Jean-Luc. It looks absolutely delicious. I'll be right back."

She grabbed her enormous purse, grateful she had brought a change of clothes, and slipped into the bathroom to brush her teeth and get dressed. Pulling on her mauve tank and the black gypsy skirt with the huge pink roses that Jean-Luc loved, she twisted her hair up into a loose topknot. And returned to her sexy chef.

As she approached the kitchen counter, Jean-Luc rose from his stool, appreciation and admiration glinting in his dark brown eyes. He pulled her into his arms. "You are exquisite, Ella. A beautiful, bohemian goddess. *Ma belle bohémienne.*" He kissed her softly, then seated her at the bar where breakfast awaited. "I love your hair like that. It reminds me of *la Belle Époque.*" His warm lips caressed the back of her neck, sending ripples of pleasure down her spine, as she settled onto the barstool next to his.

With a shy smile at his effusive compliments, Ella sampled the delectable *omelette aux épinards,* humming her approval of his culinary creation.

He's an artist, a dancer, and a fabulous cook. The way he looks at me…it makes me feel alluring. Desirable. Wanted. For the first time in my life, I feel beautiful and sexy. And when he makes love to me… God, I have never felt this attracted to a man before. I'll remember this unforgettable summer forever…

The thought of returning to her lonely apartment filled Ella with sadness and dread. *No, I won't ruin the present by worrying about the future. "Cueillez dès aujourd'hui les roses de la vie."* Ella vowed to follow the sage advice of the famous poet, Pierre de Ronsard. And pick today the roses of her life.

****

Jean-Luc knew Ella would love *le Musée de la Vie Romantique.* He watched her delighted eyes sparkle like emeralds as she took in the personal artifacts of the French writer Aurore Dupin—the rebellious female novelist who had defied convention and chosen the pen name George Sand—and her illustrious lover, the renowned pianist, Frédéric Chopin.

Ella hovered over the private collection of jewels, the marble sculpture of the famed writer, the plaster cast of George Sand's arm and her lover's legendary left hand, as well as the various *objets d'art* from the nineteenth century Romantic period in literature.

A while later, as they sat in the *Salon de Thé*—the

tearoom situated in the rose garden behind *le Musée de la Vie Romantique*— Jean-Luc marveled at Ella's enthusiasm and zest for life. She'd been delighted with the paintings, sculptures, and exhibits in the museum, and was thoroughly enjoying the ham and cheese baguette sandwiches, the *tartelettes aux fruits*, and the abundant pink roses in full bloom among the vibrant purple and blue clematis flowers that surrounded the terrace where they now sat.

After lunch, he led her along the quaint cobbled stone streets of Montmartre, watching her peruse the souvenir shops, purchasing a few postcards and books with colorful images to share with her students upon her return to Florida. He swallowed a tight lump in his throat at the thought of her leaving. Although they had only known each other for a short time, he found himself thinking of her constantly. And wanting her more and more.

They stopped by several secondhand shops, searching for vintage lace for Ella to use in designing the handmade items she sold online. "It's mostly just a hobby," she explained, "but I create what I call 'Renaissance Denim Couture'. I upcycle vintage denim into bohemian jean skirts and jackets— by adding lace, silk, velvet, and decorative beading. I don't make a lot of profit, but the added income does boost my meager teacher salary. At least a little, anyway."

Jean-Luc also found exactly what he was looking for—an antique wooden mirror with ornate, intricately carved roses. He didn't mind that the glass was cracked, for he intended to use it as a picture frame, rather than a mirror, to encase the portrait of Ella he intended to start tomorrow night. While Ella attended the evening reception at *la résidence* to welcome the arrival of the remaining teachers for the summer language and culture program, Jean-Luc would paint the portrait from the picture he'd snapped on his phone the day he'd given her the bouquet of plump peonies and pink roses. The day she'd worn the same beautiful gypsy skirt she was wearing today.

He smiled inwardly, remembering the unabashed joy on her face when she'd accepted the bouquet. The irresistible exuberance he would capture on canvas. And encase in this antique mirror which he would convert to the perfect picture frame. He couldn't wait to see the delight on her face when it was finished. And tomorrow afternoon, he'd paint her nude… The thought of her reclining on the black velvet sofa made him hard as a rock. With a stifled groan, he adjusted his clothing. And smiled at the beautiful Muse who inspired his art. And made his spirit and body sing.

"It's nearly five, and I need to set up on *la Place du Tertre* soon," he said reluctantly. "Since it's Saturday, there will be lots of tourists tonight… I'll be busy until after midnight. Too late for me to come by *la résidence*." Her face fell in disappointment. "But tomorrow, we can spend the day together again," he suggested brightly. "I have a couple more secrets of Paris to show you." He chuckled softly at the look of wonder in her widened eyes. *One of the things I adore most about her—la joie de vivre. Her contagious, exuberant joy for life.*

"I'll walk you home now." Clutching the treasured mirror against his side, Jean-Luc offered Ella the crook of his other elbow. "And pick you up tomorrow morning around ten." He led her along the quaint cobbled stone street under the dense canopy of leafy shade trees, the enticing aroma of *crêpes au chocolat* from a nearby vendor wafting through the cool spring breeze. "We'll stop by a *café* for croissants and coffee, explore Paris a bit more, then come back to the *atelier* so I can paint your portrait. Sound good?"

"Perfect. I can't wait!" She beamed at him as they walked up the path to the four-story residence nestled behind the familiar pink and green building of *la Maison Rose*.

With his free arm, he hugged her close, leaning down to envelop her soft, full lips with his own. "I wish I didn't have to work. I'd much rather make love to you …" His hand dropped to her lower back, pulling her hips against the thickened shaft which strained painfully inside his tight jeans. With considerable effort, he took a step back, withdrawing from her enticing embrace.

Lifting her hand to his lips, he whispered, "Tomorrow, *mon coeur*. I'll show you how much I crave your exquisite body."

She dazzled him with a glorious smile, then headed toward the entrance door. Unable to take his eyes off her, he watched his bohemian Muse climb the steps, enter the building, and wave goodbye through the large window.

Adjusting his clothing once again, Jean-Luc turned away. Exhaled forcefully. And walked back to the *Atelier des Lumières*.

****

Ella climbed the stairs to her private room, unlocked the door, and dropped her bags onto the small bed. She'd found two colorful posters—one of *le Sacré-Coeur* and another of *Notre-Dame*—which, along with the postcards and souvenirs, would enhance her classroom and fascinate her students. *If there's even a position for me next year*, she thought glumly. She gazed out the window at the picturesque streets of Montmartre, a sensuous thrill rippling up her spine as she envisioned the handsome, intriguing Jean-Luc. For the first time in her life, a man had made her feel desirable. Sexy. Irresistible.

He had been the only man to go ever down on her. To give her the indescribable pleasure of his skilled lips and tongue. No man had ever made her come. Or even considered her pleasure before his own. And no man had ever made her feel wanted and beautiful, the way Jean-Luc did.

The thought of leaving him— of returning to her small apartment, lonely life, and the uncertainty of the future— filled Ella with dread. *At least we have the whole month of June. Plenty of time to make utterly unforgettable memories. Unless, like all the others, including Paul—he loses interest in me.*

Shaking off her unsettling reverie, Ella showered, changed clothes, and strolled down the hall to find Yelena.

A smiling face and twinkling brown eyes greeted her knock at the door. "Come on in," Yelena welcomed Ella in French, kissing her on each cheek in the friendly, familiar greeting of *la bise.* "I've made a salad, and there's enough for two. Have a seat and tell me all about salsa dancing with Jean-Luc while I pour us some wine."

Yelena handed Ella a glass of *Sauvignon Blanc,* setting the small table with a crusty baguette, nut-encrusted goat cheese, and an enormous salad. Heaped with chunks of white tuna, fresh string beans, vine-ripened tomatoes, hard-boiled egg, sliced olives, and an incredible vinaigrette dressing with minced garlic, Ella gaped at the delectable *salade niçoise.* It looked indescribably delicious.

While they ate and sipped wine, Ella described how Jean-Luc had taught her the basics of salsa dancing, twirling her in his experienced arms to the upbeat, steady rhythm of the Latin music in the trendy *Loca Luna.* She shared the visit to *le Musée de la Vie Romantique,* how she'd found souvenirs for her classroom, and how Jean-Luc had promised to take her to discover more of the hidden secrets of Paris tomorrow.

"I must confess… I am quite jealous." Yelena chuckled, sipping her wine. "But I'm also delighted that you've met such an alluring man. An artist, a dancer…your own personal tour guide. You are very lucky indeed."

"He's an incredible lover, too." Ella savored the dry, fruity flavor of the *Sauvignon Blanc* after swallowing a bite of baguette spread with the tangy, creamy goat cheese. "I've never felt this way about any man before. Not even my husband." She smiled sadly as she traced the rim of her wineglass with the delicate tip of a long finger. "Paul was always more interested in watching whatever was on TV than in anything I had to say." She gulped a large swallow of wine, washing down the painful memories of rejection and years of neglect. "I remember once…he was watching a football game. I put on a sexy lace teddy to entice him. I got up the nerve to stand in front of the TV, hoping he'd notice. And want to make love." Ella looked down at her glass, her eyes suddenly brimming with unexpected tears. She glanced up to meet Yelena's soft, sympathetic gaze. "Do you know what he said?" With a bitter laugh that was more like a choked sob, she spat, "Move over. *I can't see the game."*

Yelena squeezed Ella's hand, her quiet companionship a soothing solace.

"Any time I wanted to speak to Paul, I'd always have to ask him if he was listening. He'd mute the TV, irritated at being interrupted. Then, after I'd said what I wanted to say, he'd just turn the volume back up. Without comment. As if nothing I said even mattered." She downed the rest of her wine. "We hardly ever made love. Only when he wanted to, and it was always over quickly. When he was finished, we were done. My satisfaction didn't matter at all."

Yelena refilled their glasses, encouraging Ella to continue with the much-needed catharsis.

Ella smiled in gratitude as she took a large swallow, the mellow warmth relaxing in Yelena's comforting presence. "But Jean-Luc is different," Ella mused as the image of his handsome face and magnificent body floated into her mind. "He's. unlike any man I've ever known. He tells me I'm beautiful, that he can't get enough of me. He's a skilled lover. And he always puts my pleasure first, before his own."

Yelena's limpid brown eyes melted like milk chocolate. "Mmm," she purred. "He sounds perfect. No wonder you're falling for him."

I am falling for him. I love everything about him. His long black hair, neatly trimmed beard, dazzling smile. His muscular chest, covered with dark hair, the tattoos on his arm and stomach. The incredible scorpion tattoo on his back, with enormous pincers curving upward like the outstretched arms of a flamenco dancer. "I'm a Scorpio," he'd confided, when her loving, explorative fingers had traced the extraordinary design emblazoned between his broad, brawny shoulders. She loved the way he had danced just for her. His unique, creative talent as an artist. And above all, she loved how he craved her, made love to her, and filled her empty soul with passion and fire. *Yes, I am definitely falling for Jean-Luc Cortés. And falling hard.*

The thought of leaving him at the end of June filled her with emptiness and sorrow.

"I have an idea. Would you like to go shopping? I saw some pretty scarves in a boutique nearby. I want to get a few postcards and souvenirs to bring home for my classroom. We can get a Nutella *crêpe*, and a cup of *chocolat chaud.*" Yelena finished her wine and flashed Ella an impish smile. "I also want to get my portrait done, like you did. We can head over to *la Place du Tertre* so that Jean-Luc can sketch me. And then, when he's done, you can go home with your sexy bohemian artist." She grinned at Ella's enthusiastic nod of approval.

"I'll pack a change of clothes. Jean-Luc said he wanted to show me a few more *secrets of Paris* tomorrow. Can you stop by my room in a few minutes when you're ready?" Ella carried the salad bowls and wine glasses into the small kitchen area. She washed and rinsed them in the sink, then placed them in the drainer on the countertop to dry.

Yelena wrapped up the goat cheese and put it, along with the vinaigrette dressing, back in the tiny refrigerator. "Sounds perfect. I'll brush my hair, grab a jacket, and be there in five minutes."

Ella dashed down the hall to her room, her spirit soaring at the thought of spending the night with Jean-Luc. With a sudden pang of self-doubt, she wondered if he might not be glad to see her. He might have made other plans. Maybe even with another woman. *Stop it! You'll be able to tell if he's glad to see you when Yelena gets her portrait sketched. If he seems preoccupied or uninterested, then you'll you know. He might very well be delighted. Just wait and see.*

Tamping down her nagging insecurities, Ella decided to wear one of her Renaissance Denim Couture creations—a snug, faded jean skirt with pale pink rose lace appliqués curving along both sides of the corset-like lacing. Layers of mauve lace and shimmery silk ruffles cascaded in a sexy but chic asymmetrical hemline that fell almost to her ankle on one side and bared her knee on the other. *Jean-Luc loves my long legs. This skirt will flutter as I walk. And give him a great view.*

She wore her hair down—for he loved it that way—and packed her makeup, toothbrush, and a long bohemian skirt in shades of turquoise and teal with a matching top into a huge black bag. After a quick mental inventory, confident she'd included everything she'd need for tomorrow, she hoisted the embellished bag over her shoulder. Greeted Yelena's expected knock at the door. And headed out into the starry night sky and the irresistible lure of Montmartre.

Inside a little boutique, Yelena held up a floral scarf and raised her eyebrows inquisitively. "Do you like this one?" The shades of lilac and deep purple complemented her coloring and highlighted her expressive brown eyes.

Ella smiled encouragingly as Yelena looked in the mirror. "It's gorgeous. I love it."

"Ooh," Yelena gasped as she spotted a slouchy bohemian bag adorned with amethyst-colored crystals and sparkly lavender beads. "This will match it perfectly."

The pretty scarf draped around her neck and the new purse slung over her shoulder, an exuberant Yelena led Ella to a glass kiosk where the delicious aroma of crêpes perfumed the vibrant night air. She ordered them each a Nutella crêpe, and Ella watched in awe as the vendor poured a ladle of thin batter into the sizzling pan, flipped the thin pancake high into the air, and caught it perfectly to lightly brown the other side. Topping the warm crêpe with a generous dollop of Nutella, he folded it expertly with his spatula, slid it onto a sheet of wax paper, wrapped it up and handed it to Yelena. He then repeated the fascinating performance and gave Ella hers.

"Mmm," she hummed, as she bit into the warm crêpe, the gooey goodness of melted Nutella a decadent mouthful of chocolate hazelnut bliss. "This is *delicious.*"

They ate every sumptuous bite, licked their sticky fingers, and tossed the empty wrappers in the nearby trashcan. Yelena checked the time on her phone. A mischievous glint sparked in her dark eyes. "Come on, let's go get my portrait sketched."

Amid the familiar red umbrellas and lush canopy of shade trees, *La Place du Tertre* was bustling with tourists. Some were seated, having their portrait sketched, others perused the various works of art for sale, and many mingled, reveling in the lively ambience of bohemian Paris.

Ella spotted Jean-Luc across the cobbled stone square. Clad in his usual black tee shirt and tattered, faded jeans, his long hair was tied back in a queue, his expression serious as he concentrated on sketching the portrait of a middle-aged woman whose husband was watching with an approving smile. A young woman stood next in line, patiently waiting her turn, while several other potential customers admired his collection of paintings.

At Yelena and Ella's approach, Jean-Luc raised his gaze. As his eyes met hers, a dazzling smile stretched across his handsome face, illuminating Ella's entire soul.

He set down his piece of charcoal, excused himself politely from his customers for just a moment. And enveloped Ella in his tattooed, chiseled arms. Warm lips brushed hers as he whispered into her mouth. "I am so glad you're here. I've been thinking about you all night. Can you stay? And come home with me later?"

Ella wrapped her arms around his neck, overcome with joy. "Yes. I would love to."

Releasing her with a glorious grin, he stepped back to welcome Yelena.

"Hi, Jean-Luc," she said, kissing his cheeks in greeting. "I'd love to have you sketch my portrait, when you've finished theirs," she said, gesturing to his waiting customers. "We'll wait until you're available... and browse through your work."

Jean-Luc nodded and returned to his clients. A few moments later, the couple departed, satisfied with their charcoal portrait.

While he sketched the young woman, Yelena admired Jean-Luc's talent as she and Ella examined the displayed pieces. "I love this one," she exclaimed, indicating a painting of five female flamenco dancers with vibrant costumes in alternating colors of yellow and red. "He's captured the fluidity of movement with the unfurling ruffles of their dresses. The intensity of emotion in their facial expressions. The power and passion of flamenco. I'm going to buy it. And every time

I look at it, I'll remember the performance we saw. When Jean-Luc danced *just for you.*"

Ella's stomach somersaulted at the memory. Jean-Luc's powerful legs. His feet stomping and prancing like a wild stallion. The flick of his long mane, drenching her with droplets of sweat. Making love to her through his dance. Liquid fire pooled between her thighs.

When he'd completed the portrait of his last customer, Jean-Luc beckoned Yelena to come forward.

She handed him the painting she'd selected, settled into the folding chair, and smiled knowingly at Ella while he worked his magic with charcoal on the paper stretched across his canvas. Half an hour later, when he presented the completed portrait, Yelena glowed in delight, praising his work effusively.

Jean-Luc rolled her portrait carefully inside protective paper, then slipped an elastic band around the outside to secure it tightly. Wrapping her painting of the flamenco dancers as well, he tucked both works of art inside a paper bag with handles for her to carry home. He swept her debit card and thanked her for the two purchases. As she signed her name across his phone, he announced with a nod to the painter nearby, "I'll ask Gérard to keep an eye on my things while Ella and I walk you home."

After escorting Yelena back to *la résidence*, Jean-Luc and Ella returned to *la Place du Tertre* to pack up his supplies. "I'm so glad you came here tonight. I wanted you to spend the night with me, but midnight is much too late for me to come knocking on your door. This is perfect." He pulled her close, brushing his lips softly against hers. "Now we can make love. And sleep in each other's arms." The tip of his tongue traced the silky lining inside her mouth, sending warm waves of pleasure rippling to her core.

Ella's legs weakened with desire.

As Jean-Luc locked the door to the apartment behind them, Ella set down the bags she'd carried back to the *Atelier des Lumières*. He placed a stack of paintings in the corner, washed his hands in the nearby sink. And led Ella up the wooden stairs, through the double French doors. To the sumptuous bed bathed in moonlight.

"I thought about you *all night*," he whispered in her ear as his lips trailed kisses along her throat. He lifted her black top up over her arms, baring her small breasts.

Quivering in anticipation, Ella's entire body twitched and trembled.

As warm, insistent lips engulfed her swollen nipples, creating a throbbing ache between her thighs, Jean-Luc pushed her jean skirt and lace panties down her hips to puddle on the floor. While she stood nude, shaking with desire, he removed his black tee shirt, and Ella ran her fingers through the hair across his chest.

He unzipped his jeans, and Ella followed the dark trail down his abdomen, her appreciative gaze resting on his ardent arousal. Taking her hand, he led her to the bed and laid her down gently. He pushed her thighs wide, moaning as he parted her wet folds with trembling fingers and lowered his eager mouth to lap, lick, and slurp her luscious wet lips.

Ella gripped the sheets as her leg muscles tightened, the intense pleasure almost unbearable torture.

"God, I want you," he groaned, positioning himself between her quavering thighs. The tip of his engorged cock poked and prodded, seeking entrance and promised relief from the agonizing ache.

Slipping his calloused hands under her receptive hips, he tilted her pelvis up. And plunged them both into paradise.

Ella wrapped her arms around his broad back, her legs around his pulsing hips, pulling him deeper inside as she matched his pumping thrusts. Tighter and tighter she gripped him, the tension mounting to an excruciating peak, until he arched and burrowed into her, filling her depths with liquid fire.

Rhythmic contractions and waves of exquisite pleasure rocked Ella as her body clenched his, squeezing and extracting every drop as he convulsed and shuddered within her entwined limbs.

He exhaled in audible relief. "I needed that. God, it was *intense*." He suckled her shoulder, lifted himself off her, and rolled onto his back.

Ella lowered her twitching legs, the pleasure of afterglow flowing through her sated body. She smiled up at Jean-Luc's shining eyes, glimmering in the moonlight.

He drew her into his open, welcoming arms. "M*on coeur*," he murmured, wrapping her up in a snug embrace and pulling her gently onto his chest. He kissed her hair and whispered softly. "Come… sleep upon my heart."

Chapter 6

Enflammée

Early summer sunlight filtered through the arched window as Ella's eyelids fluttered awake. The enticing aroma of fresh coffee filled the air as she stretched her long limbs across the bed, purring like a contented cat. In the kitchen, she glimpsed Jean-Luc's naked torso, the scorpion tattoo with enormous pincers twirling up his broad back like the curved arms of a flamboyant flamenco dancer.

He'd set the countertop for breakfast, with fresh squeezed orange juice, two *bols de café,* and four pastries on a pretty platter nestled between two small plates in the same turquoise hue. *"Pain au chocolat,"* he grinned, gesturing to the flaky rolls. "My favorite."

Ella stood up, stretched her arms overhead, and flashed Jean-Luc an appreciative smile. "It looks wonderful. I'll be right back." She quickly made the bed and slipped into the bathroom. A few minutes later, she emerged with a freshly scrubbed face, clean teeth, and brushed hair. After a quick deliberation, she decided to remain nude and slipped onto the barstool beside Jean-Luc.

Appreciation and desire dancing in his dark eyes, he swiveled her chair to face him, parting her knees with his own. Leaning forward to claim her lips, he growled in a ragged, husky voice. "You look good enough to *eat*." He slid off his chair, moving it back a bit as he dropped to his knees between her open thighs. Pulling her to the edge of the seat, he feasted on her delicate folds. And— as she clutched the counter for balance, succumbing to his skilled lips and tongue—made Ella come in her chair.

"Best breakfast I've ever had," he smirked, licking his lips for exaggerated effect. As he unzipped and removed his jeans, his erect cook sprang to life. Sitting onto the barstool, using the countertop for support against his back, he lifted Ella onto his lap. Straddled her over his muscular thighs. And, lifting her up and down as he plunged in deep, made her ride him like a galloping stallion.

When they'd recovered, he helped her to the floor as she regained her footing on unsteady, wobbly legs.

With a grin, he handed her a paper napkin as he wiped himself with another before pulling on his jeans. "I can't get enough of you, Ella. I want you all the time."

She tossed her used napkin into the trash, then wrapped her arms around his waist. Burying her nose into the dark hair on his chest, she inhaled his tangy, distinctly male scent deep into her lungs. "Me, too. I feel the same."

He raised her chin with a curved finger and kissed her softly. "Let's eat. I want to show you more of the hidden secrets of Paris."

****

Rows of vines bursting with grapes lined the steep slopes of *la butte*—the hill of Montmartre—as Jean-Luc led Ella to the summit. "This is *Le Clos Montmartre*," he explained with a smile. "The vineyard of Montmartre. It dates back to the Middle Ages, but these vines were replanted in 1933, just before the French government imposed all the rules and regulations for wine production." He gazed out at the leafy plants laden with fruit. "Every October, Montmartre has a huge festival – *La Fête des Vendanges*—to celebrate the annual harvest. There's music, dancing, parades, exhibits… all sorts of revelry. And an auction to sell the wine, with the proceeds going to charity. I've bought us tickets to tour the museum today. It even includes a wine tasting. Come, let me show you another of the secret delights of Paris."

As she and Jean-Luc accompanied the tour guide to view the collections of art in *le Musée de Montmartre,* Ella learned that this bohemian district of Paris had once been a mecca for revolutionary painters, rebellious writers, innovative musicians, and free thinkers. Beginning in the Romantic era with George Sand, Frédéric Chopin, and Victor Hugo, continuing through *la Belle Époque*— when Impressionists such as Toulouse-Lautrec, Vincent Van Gogh and Pierre-Auguste Renoir painted here—and into the twentieth century with Picasso and Utrillo, Montmartre had always attracted the world's most illustrious artists.

Renoir had lived and painted here, the guide explained as they strolled through the lush gardens where Ella spotted the swing which had inspired his famous painting, *La Balançoire.* The tour concluded with a delightful wine tasting and the gift of a glass engraved with the name *Le Clos Montmartre*.

Another memorable souvenir of an unforgettable summer. Ella tucked the precious memento in her black velvet hobo bag, accepted Jean-Luc's outstretched hand, and strolled with her bohemian artist back down the hill of Montmartre.

"Let's pick up a couple sandwiches and go back to the atelier. I want to paint you." Jean-Luc grinned, lifting her hand to his smiling lips.

"That sounds fantastic. But I need to be back at *la résidence* by five. There's a reception planned for us tonight at *la Maison Rose*—to welcome the teachers, allow us to introduce ourselves, and meet the directors of the program. They'll give us the overview of classes, excursions, and expectations. It's from six till nine." Ella smiled as he squeezed her hand.

"Then I'll come pick you up at *la Maison Rose* at nine. We'll go to the cabaret, *Au Lapin Agile.* Tonight, they're performing classic songs by Édith Piaf, Jacques Brel, and Charles Aznavour. A flashback to times gone by. You'll love it. Another delightful secret of Montmartre…"

Ella's spirit soared as they sauntered along the quaint cobbled stone street toward *l'Atelier des Lumières.*

I never want this unforgettable summer to end.

With a bittersweet smile, she sighed, swallowing a lump of sadness at the thought of returning home.

Of leaving Montmartre.

And facing the inevitable, unbearable sorrow of losing Jean-Luc.

****

A cordial hostess escorted Ella and Yelena into the private banquet room of *la Maison Rose* reserved for the French teachers who had arrived for the summer language and culture program in Montmartre. As they sat at tables adorned with white linens and fragrant bouquets of spring flowers, the twenty-four participants were greeted by the four professors who would be their instructors for the month of June while waiters served appetizers, fresh bread, and glasses of rich red wine.

"Good evening, everyone. Welcome to the Art in Montmartre Summer Immersion Program for Teachers of French as a Foreign Language. I am Jacques Dubois, *le Directeur*, and I wish to welcome you all. Tonight, we'll inform you of the classes and planned cultural excursions...and have the opportunity to introduce ourselves and get to know one another. But first, let's enjoy this splendid dinner prepared for us by *la Maison Rose*. Again, welcome, everyone. Enjoy the fine French cuisine. *Bon appétit*."

Over the course of the evening, Ella learned that the teachers had been divided into two groups of twelve to attend alternating classes from nine to noon three days a week, with excursions to various museums on Tuesday and Thursday mornings. Afternoons, evenings, and weekends were free to explore Paris, with an optional trip to Giverny offered midway through the program. A *médiathèque*—complete with books, magazines, computers, and Internet access—was located on the ground floor of *la résidence*. All program participants would prepare a midterm and final multimedia presentation of art in Montmartre, to be used in their French classrooms upon return to their respective home countries.

After the reception, Ella said goodbye to Sofía and Carmen—two new teacher friends from Argentina—and promised to meet Yelena in the morning so they could walk to class together.

"Have fun with Jean-Luc," Yelena whispered as she kissed Ella's cheeks with *la bise* of farewell. "See you tomorrow."

Her breath hitched at the sight of his handsome, grinning face as Ella exited the restaurant. *He is by far the most beautiful man I have ever seen.* Once again, the venomous voice slithered into her mind. *He'll lose interest, like Paul. It's just a matter of time.* Shaking her head to dispel the self-doubt, Ella waltzed into Jean-Luc's awaiting embrace.

****

The first two weeks of classes flew by. As Ella learned more about the history of Montmartre, she remembered the trip to *le Musée de la Vie Romantique* and the delightful vineyard visit with Jean-Luc. During the excursion to the *Musée d' Orsay*, she was fascinated by the former train station transformed into a museum for Impressionist art, discovering the characteristic joy in the rosy, cherubic faces of Renoir's famous portraits. The torturous twirls of fiery flames and the spiral swirls of starry skies in Van Gogh's masterpieces. The ephemeral, incomparable water lilies of Monet's *nymphéas.* And, when she finally viewed the famous sculpture of *le Penseur,* Ella marveled at Rodin's incomparable ability to create the lifelike Thinker from a giant slab of hard white marble with a mere chisel.

And yet—as much as she enjoyed immersing herself into the French language and culture, Ella constantly thought of Jean-Luc. She compared every work of art to his. The flamenco dancers whose passion and pain evoked the intensity of Van Gogh's emotion. The vivid colors and bold shapes of Matisse and Picasso. The intimate portraits of performers, like the famed ballerinas of Degas, or the burlesque cabaret singers of Toulouse-Lautrec.

Indeed, her talented bohemian artist was always on her mind.

They spent as much time together as possible. During the week, he picked her up at *la résidence* after classes, and they'd share lunch, strolling along the shady streets of Montmartre, returning to the apartment to make love in his luxurious bed. On the evenings when he sketched portraits on *la Place du Tertre,* Ella did aerobics in her room, studied in the *médiathèque*, or went souvenir shopping with Yelena. On the nights when Jean-Luc danced, Ella met him at the *Tablao Flamenco* and went home with him after the performance. They had afternoons, Wednesday nights, and weekends together. And all day every Sunday.

Today, while Ella and Jean-Luc shared *sandwiches au poulet* on a pretty park bench under a canopy of leafy trees, she told him about the midterm presentation she'd given that morning about Renoir's famous works. "I talked about *la joie de vivre* in his portraits. The happy faces and joyous ambiance of *la Belle Époque*. I mentioned our guided tour of *le Musée de Montmartre*," she said between bites of her chicken baguette sandwich. "And compared the two paintings Renoir completed while living there. I think it went very well."

Jean-Luc smiled enthusiastically, pleased with her success. But he seemed preoccupied and restless, as if eager to share important news. As they walked back to the apartment along the *Allée des Brouillards*, near the vineyard they'd visited on the tour of *le Clos Montmartre*, he wrapped an arm around her shoulder and, with a sweeping gesture of his other arm, indicated the abundant shade trees and lush vegetation lining both sides of the quiet street. "I'd love to live here, like Renoir did. A peaceful, private oasis. Right in the heart of Montmartre."

That's one of the things I love best about Paris. It's a huge city, with enchanting places like this. A composite collection of quaint little towns.

When they arrived at the atelier, Jean-Luc led Ella upstairs, his face as eager as a child on Christmas morning. As she walked through the double French doors into the foyer of the apartment, her mouth dropped open. There, on the recessed wall between the open living/bedroom area and the small kitchen, centered above his computer desk, was a portrait of Ella. Holding the bouquet of plump pink peonies and roses that Jean-Luc had given her. The day they'd sat among the wisteria blossoms near *le Sacré-Coeur*.

He'd taken the broken mirror they'd found in the thrift shop, painted it black, and transformed it into an ornate picture frame with intricately carved roses. The mauve matting he'd placed inside the antique frame was the same shade of soft pink as the roses clutched in Ella's hands and in the floral spray scattered across her long black gypsy skirt. Hair upswept into a loose *pompadour,* soft tendrils delicately framing her face, emerald eyes sparkling with unabashed delight— Jean-Luc had intimately captured that moment of Ella's exquisite joy. Just like the illustrious Impressionist artists of the beautiful *Belle Époque*.

With an awestruck intake of breath, Ella rushed over to examine the painting more closely. The black and pink colors of the mat and frame highlighted the hues of her skirt, and the carved roses in the former mirror perfectly complemented the flowers in the bouquet. "It's beautiful. I absolutely *love* it!"

Jean-Luc walked up behind her, wrapped his arms around the front of her waist, and brushed his lips along the side of her neck. "I call it *Ma Rose Bohème.* My bohemian rose. " The tip of his tongue traced the shell of her ear. "Now, I can look at you every day." He spun her around to face him. Yearning blazed in his dark, intense gaze. "You're my Muse, Ella. The inspiration for my art. My passion. My joy. *Mon coeur.*" He crushed her against his chest, resting his head protectively upon hers. "I wish you didn't have to go back to Florida. I want you to stay here with me."

He gently raised her chin, his impassioned eyes searing her soul. With a guttural groan, his mouth claimed hers, penetrating her parted lips with a probing, insistent tongue. As he delved deep, Jean-Luc backed her up against the wall, hoisted her skirt around her waist, and dropped his jeans to his knees.

Ella gasped at the sight of the huge shaft that would soon penetrate her like a sword. A jolt of liquid desire surged between her shaking thighs. She wrapped her arms around Jean-Luc's shoulders and her legs around his waist as he lifted her off the floor.

Gripping her in a frantic, desperate hold, he pinned her against the wall. Plunged inside her, pummeling mercilessly until she screamed in release. And filled her— body and soul— with fiery, liquid flames.

Later, they sat in the kitchen, sharing the quiet grilled shrimp dinner that Jean-Luc had prepared. He refilled their glasses of *Meursault*, then placed the wine bottle back in the ice bucket beside him. "A week from today is *La Fête de la Musique.* Every year, each city in France celebrates the Festival of Music on June 21st. Here in Montmartre, there'll be festivities near *le Sacré-*

Coeur. I'm glad it falls on a Wednesday, so we can spend the whole afternoon and evening together." He flashed her a sly grin, a mischievous glint dancing in his dark eyes. "I'm almost finished with your nude portrait. I'll show it to that day. You can express your gratitude..." he chuckled deeply, leaning over to plant his lips on hers. "And after that, we'll dance in the streets and celebrate *la Fête de la Musique.*"

The summer program is almost over. Soon, I'll have to fly home. And leave Jean-Luc. Ella smiled at his suggestions for the upcoming celebration. But her spirit was heavy with loss.

When Jean-Luc picked her up at *la résidence* the following Wednesday after classes ended, they strolled to the pretty square near *le Sacré-Coeur* where the wisteria bloomed among the leafy shady trees. Jazz music wafted through the air, a mellow saxophone augmenting Ella's melancholy mood.

She'd been especially moved during today's lecture about Picasso's famous painting, *La Mort de Casagemas*, completed during the Blue Period just after the suicide of his close friend. As she and Jean-Luc savored their *sandwiches au poulet*, Ella shared the sad story. "Picasso's friend killed himself because he couldn't have Germaine, the woman he loved. Such a tragic death."

Jean-Luc grasped Ella's hand and raised it to his sensuous lips. "*L'amour fou.* A passion so intense... it can drive you mad." Flames of golden sunlight blazed in his fierce, feral eyes.

His scorching lips gently sucked at her knuckles.

And Ella's nipples ached, longing for their touch.

As if he'd read her thoughts, Jean-Luc crumpled the

wax paper that their sandwiches had been wrapped in, arose from the green wooden bench where they both sat, and tossed their trash into the receptacle under the verdant canopy of a huge oak. He returned to her side. Offered his hand. And briskly led her—amid myriad music soaring into the sky— back to the *Atelier des Lumières*.

Instead of going upstairs to the bedroom, as Ella had hoped, Jean-Luc escorted her down the hall to his spacious studio. Dense foliage covering the exterior privacy wall sheltered the floor to ceiling window where dappled sunlight filtered through the leaves onto the gleaming pinewood floor. Ella's eyes roved over the familiar black velvet sofa— where she and Jean-Luc had made love during every session that she had posed for him— before settling onto the wall where a large sheet covered the painting he was most anxious to show her.

"Today is *la Fête de la Musique*. And your portrait is finished, like I promised." With theatrical *panache,* he unveiled his masterpiece. And Ella's jaw dropped to her chest.

He'd painted her reclining seductively on the sumptuous divan, accentuating the sleek, sinuous lines of her long, lithe legs. Her left arm was tucked up under her head, and a perk pink nipple protruded from the cascade of golden tresses tumbling over her shoulder to the sharp, sensuous curve of her full, rounded hip. Lips parted slightly, eyes glazed with desire, Ella sizzled with pure, provocative passion. The effect was electrifying.

Stunned speechless, Ella stood agape, gawking at the nude image of herself. She looked alluring and exotic. Decadent and desirable. Bewitching, beguiling, and beautiful.

This is how he sees me. Unlike any man ever has before.

"*Enflammée,*" he whispered into her ear as he crept up behind her. "Engulfed in flames." Hot lips clamped her shoulder, intently sucking her soft skin. "The fiery passion that fuels my soul. Inspires my art. And makes my heart sing."

Ella's legs gave out, and he caught her with strong, sinewy arms. She slumped forward— for he was behind her— succumbing to his insistent, urgent mouth.

He kicked her legs apart, bent her roughly over the nearby table, and hoisted her skirt up over her back.

A piercing pleasure tore her apart as he arrowed into her. Calloused hands clenched her hips in a tight, immovable grip. Powerful thighs slammed the back of her legs. Pounding, vigorous thrusts rammed her to the hilt. When the mounting tension crested to an irresistible, impossible peak, Ella grabbed hold of the sides of the table. And catapulted into the abyss.

Breath heaving, Jean-Luc withdrew from her body ."*L'amour fou,*" he gasped, pulling Ella into his arms. "My passion for you is so intense… it makes me lose my mind."

She wrapped her trembling arms around his broad back, nuzzling the dark hair that traversed his chest and trailed down his quivering abs. His musky scent stirred her senses and called to her very soul. *No man has ever said that to me. Or made me feel so alive.*

"I don't want you to leave," he murmured, enveloping her in a tight embrace. Afternoon sunlight gilded the golden flecks in his dark, possessive eyes. "I've given it a lot of thought," he said, kissing her softly on the lips. "You could delay your flight…and stay here with me. For at least the month of July."

Ella couldn't breathe. Her heart had flown out of her chest.

"You're a language teacher. Instead of teaching French in the United States, you could give English lessons here. There's a huge demand for it in Paris." He gazed down at her, his handsome face alight with hope. "We can put a sign in the window of my shop, and recruit clients to sign up for your classes. So that, when your program ends next week, you'll have a source of income to help pay your rent in Florida."

His convincing gaze held hers. "If no job offer materializes... you could stay here with me. *Indefinitely.*"

Ella shook with emotion. *I wouldn't need to leave Jean-Luc. He wants me to stay!*

His deep voice picked up momentum. "You could sell the jean skirts you make—the Renaissance Denim Couture. We can get you a sewing machine. Set you up in a corner of the living room upstairs. You can find vintage jeans and lace in thrift shops. Display your finished creations in the window. And sell them in here in the shop. You'll have custom orders... make a decent profit. And maybe...you'll stay in Montmartre. *With me.*"

Ella threw her arms around his neck, too overcome to speak. After a moment, she took a deep breath and exclaimed, bursting with joy, "I would love to stay here with you. I've been dreading next week. Flying home to my empty apartment. Leaving you and Montmartre behind." She kissed the dense hair on his chest, inhaling his scent deep into her lungs. "Now, I look forward to the future. And living here with you."

Exuberant, filled with renewed hope, Ella straightened her rumpled skirt. Brushed her tousled hair. And, hand in hand with her bohemian flamenco dancer, went out to celebrate *la Fête de la Musique.*

****

For her final presentation in the summer immersion program for teachers, Ella compared *La Alma*——the painting of the flamenco dancer she'd bought from Jean-Luc on *la Place du Tertre* the first night she had arrived in Paris—with the vivid color and intense passion of Vincent Van Gogh's famous works, and the intimate portrayal of performers in the masterpieces of Edgar Degas and Toulouse-Lautrec. The enthusiastic response from her colleagues and professors was the highlight of the last week of classes.

The farewell dinner took place in the same private banquet room of *la Maison Rose* where the teachers had been welcomed at the start of the program. Ella profusely thanked her instructors and *les moniteurs* who had organized the cultural excursions to the various museums. She exchanged contact information with several new friends, including Carmen and Sofía from Argentina, promising to keep in touch through social media and email.

With tears in her eyes and a lump in her throat, Ella hugged Yelena goodbye.

And—rolling her suitcase across the cobbled stone square of Montmartre—went home with Jean-Luc to the *Atelier des Lumières.*

Chapter 7

La Fête des Vendanges

Jean-Luc had been right. There was indeed a high demand for English lessons in Paris, and Ella quickly recruited a dozen clients. She established three classes of four students who met twice a week for hour-long sessions in the small studio where Jean-Luc gave his art lessons on alternate days. All of her adult students had studied English in school to varying degrees, and Ella was able to teach them not only conversational skills, but American culture as well.

She and Jean-Luc had found a sewing machine, and Ella had carved a nook in a corner of the bedroom where she created couture. She loved finding vintage denim, antique lace, and sparkly embellishments in nearby thrift shops, returning to the *Atelier des Lumières* to work upstairs while Jean-Luc greeted customers and sold paintings in his workshop on the lower level. Ella was thrilled to have already sold two jackets and four skirts, with orders for several more custom pieces of Renaissance Denim Couture.

Every afternoon, like many merchants in Paris, Jean-Luc closed his shop for lunch. And frequently made love to Ella in the sumptuous black bed. Although he worked five nights a week—dancing at the *tablao* or sketching on *la Place du Tertre*—they had afternoons,

Wednesday evenings, Saturdays…and every glorious Sunday together.

Ella finally received notice that the French teaching position she had been hoping for had been filled by a tenured instructor requesting a school transfer. Since Ella now had no job to go back to, she rescheduled her return flight for late August—within the required ninety days of her arrival in France.

Jean-Luc accompanied her to the *Préfecture de Paris,* where Ella completed an application for an extended visa, which would allow her to remain in France for another six months. If granted, Ella could remain in Montmartre with Jean-Luc and decide whether to renew the lease on her apartment in late November or apply for a *Visa de Long Séjour,* which would allow her to remain in France for an additional year.

In her heart, Ella knew she wouldn't want to renew her lease. She had no desire to go back to Florida. For the first time in her life, she felt wanted and needed. She was blissfully happy with Jean-Luc.

And in love with the vibrant bohemian life of Montmartre.

****

One Tuesday afternoon, while Ella hunted for treasures in local antique shops, Jean-Luc sat at the computer in his atelier downstairs, pouring over ledgers and inventory of supplies. At the sound of someone entering his shop, he looked up to find his landlord, Alphonse Béchamel, accompanied by a striking brunette whose ultra-chic hairstyle and impeccable clothing exuded power, position, and prestige.

"Bonjour, Jean-Luc," Alphonse said with a cordial grin and a firm handshake. "I'd like you to meet Colette

Ducharme, curator of the upcoming exhibition for *le Musée de Montmartre,* scheduled to coincide with *la Fête des Vendanges* in October. She and I recently met at a fundraiser for the annual event, and when she mentioned this year's theme—*L' Art de la Danse*—I immediately thought of you." He smiled politely at his female companion. "I'll leave you two to discuss the details. And meet you for lunch at noon." He kissed Colette's elegant, bejeweled hand. "*À bientôt.*" With another handshake and a friendly nod, Alphonse said goodbye to his astounded tenant. "*Au revoir, Jean-Luc. Bonne journée.*"

Jean-Luc watched Alphonse exit the atelier, then turned to welcome Colette Ducharme. "Would you like a cup of coffee?" he asked hospitably, offering her the chair beside his with a gallant sweep of his arm.

"No, thank you, Jean-Luc," she replied, tucking her tailored skirt with a flawlessly manicured hand as she settled onto the red velvet tufted chair.

Jean-Luc smiled hesitantly as he lowered himself onto his seat. *Why is she here?* Adrenaline coursing through his veins, he swallowed forcefully to calm his jittery nerves.

"When Alphonse mentioned that you painted flamenco dancers, I was intrigued." Colette glanced admiringly at the paintings displayed on the walls of the atelier. "My colleagues——Olivier and Guillaume—— perused your work last week when they stopped by this studio. They also observed you sketching on *la Place du Tertre.*" Colette's dark eyes glittered like black obsidian jewels. "Alphonse had told the three of us that you were a dancer yourself, so my associates and I attended the performance last Friday night at the *Tablao Flamenco.*"

Her ruby red lips curled upward in practiced, polished perfection. "You were most impressive. No wonder you're able to capture the passion and precision of flamenco in your work."

Jean-Luc wondered where all this was leading as he wiped damp palms along the side of his jeans. "Thank you," he murmured uncertainly.

"This year's exposition at *le Musée de Montmartre* will be held in October during the *la Fête des Vendanges*," Colette crooned, flashing Jean-Luc an utterly beguiling smile. "As Alphonse mentioned, the theme is *L'Art de la Danse,* and we plan to promote local artists who portray dance in their work." Her pretty white teeth sparkled in the soft, streaming rays of summer sunlight. "I'm here today to invite you, Jean-Luc Cortés, to exhibit your exquisite paintings of flamenco dancers in our unique exposition. As the featured artist of this year's event."

Jean-Luc's pulse hammered in his throat. Nearly four hundred thousand people flocked to Montmartre each year for *la Fête des Vendanges*. For him to be the featured artist of the exhibit would mean incredible publicity and exposure. Contacts with art connoisseurs throughout Europe. Increased sales and recognition. Fortune and fame.

"I'm honored, Madame Ducharme," Jean-Luc stammered, at a total loss for words.

"It's *Mademoiselle*," she corrected him coquettishly. "But please... call me Colette." She gracefully smoothed the sides of her impeccable, unwrinkled skirt. "I would also like to commission you to paint my portrait. The keynote work of art for the exhibition."

In response to the inquisitive lift of his brow, Colette laughed sweetly and replied with an impish smile. "I used to study ballet. I'd like for you to paint me in an elegant, ethereal pose. And entitle the work *L'Art de la Danse*. The name of this year's theme."

Jean-Luc shifted awkwardly under her shrewd, assessing stare. "It would be my pleasure, Madame. Euh… Colette."

"Excellent," she cooed with a smug, satisfied grin, retrieving her cellphone from a designer handbag and consulting the calendar. "You must complete the portrait by the third week of August. I'm scheduling a publicity shoot and press conference at the museum on the twenty-eighth, to promote the event and generate interest in the exhibition." Her eager eyes glinted with glee. "And you, of course—the featured artist——will be interviewed and photographed as a talented painter and flamenco dancer. It will be tremendous publicity for your work. For this *Atelier des Lumières,*" she said, gesturing to the studio around them. "*And for the Tablao Flamenco, where you perform.*" Colette leaned forward, piercing Jean-Luc with a penetrating stare. "How soon can you begin my portrait? I'd like to start right away."

Jean-Luc did a few quick mental calculations. He'd have to work afternoons and weekends…but just for a few weeks. He'd finish Colette's portrait. Do the press conferences and publicity interviews. And, if all went well, Ella's application for the extended visa would be approved. She'd be here for *la Fête des Vendanges*. And share it all with him.

"We could schedule portrait sessions each afternoon, from two to four. And Saturdays from noon to three," he offered with an encouraging smile. *I'll still have nights and Sundays with Ella. Not as much time as I'd like, but we'll make it work.*

"Perfect. I'll have mornings for meetings and necessary conferences. And spend afternoons here with you. Let's begin tomorrow at two." She tucked her cellphone into the chic black purse on her lap and arose from her chair, signaling her intent to depart. "It was a pleasure to meet you, Jean-Luc. I have the highest expectations for this year's event. *L'Art de la Danse* will be an unprecedented success."

Jean-Luc rose to his feet and shook Colette's elegantly extended hand. "Thank you very much for this incredible opportunity. I'm honored beyond measure to be the featured artist." He escorted the charming curator to the door of his atelier. "I look forward to painting your portrait. And working closely with you for *la Fête des Vendanges*." He gallantly opened the door with a chivalrous smile. "*Au revoir*, Colette. I'll see you tomorrow at two."

****

Ella swept into the workshop, thrilled at having found exactly what she needed for an elaborate custom order. As she proudly displayed the exquisite lace and distressed jeans on the table for Jean-Luc to see, she knew that his joyous, effusive exuberance indicated much more than mere interest in her treasured discovery.

He could barely contain his exhilaration. "My landlord Alphonse stopped by today, while you were shopping." He took hold of Ella's hands, drawing her attention away from the table and pulling her close. "He introduced me to his guest, Colette Ducharme, the curator of this year's art exhibition at *le Musée de Montmartre.*"

Ella absorbed Jean-Luc's contagious enthusiasm.

"The exhibit will take place in October, during *La Fête des Vendanges*. This year's theme is *L'Art de la Danse,* with collections by local artists who portray dance in their work." Deep voice quavering with emotion, his impassioned eyes transfixed hers. "Colette Ducharme wants me to be the featured artist of the entire event! She invited me to display my paintings of flamenco dancers. She commissioned me to paint her portrait... which will be the keynote piece of the exhibit. She's arranging interviews, a press conference, a publicity shoot. Ella, it's the opportunity of a lifetime!" He swept her up into his arms, swirling and twirling in breathless delight, dancing her across the atelier floor.

Setting her gently down, he wrapped his arms around her waist and pulled Ella snugly against his chest. "I hope your visa is approved, so you'll be here with me. I want to share it all with you." Soft, sensuous lips brushed hers. "You're *ma rose bohème. Mon coeur.* My Muse."

Ella knew that tonight was Jean-Luc's turn to sketch on *la Place du Tertre.* "I'll fix dinner while you get ready for work," she said affably, withdrawing from his embrace. As Jean-Luc strode down the hall to assemble his art supplies, Ella went upstairs with a cheerful grin and an upbeat mood.

The following day, Ella worked absentmindedly on her custom order, trying to focus on the fabulous antique lace she'd been so thrilled to find in the vintage shop. But, despite her best efforts to concentrate on her sewing, she kept thinking of Jean-Luc painting Colette Ducharme's portrait in the studio downstairs. Desperate to catch a glimpse of his all-important client, Ella decided to rearrange the display in the storefront window. That way, when the session ended at four, she'd be able to meet the curator who had made her bohemian artist's dreams come true.

At the sound of a deep, hearty chuckle and a lovely, lilting laugh, Ella turned toward Jean-Luc and his female companion as they exited his studio and headed toward the door.

Ella's stomach fell to the floor.

Colette Ducharme was drop dead gorgeous.

Glossy, blue-black hair was styled in a chic, sleek bob. The plunging neckline of her stretchy, amethyst top offered an alluring view of ample *décolletage*. Dark designer denim hugged her rounded hips, accentuating her tiny waist. Drawing attention to the voluptuous triangle between her sculpted, sensuous thighs.

An exuberant grin stretched across Jean-Luc's tanned, handsome face. "Ella, I'd like you to meet Colette Ducharme, the curator of this year's exhibition for *La Fête des Vendanges.*" He smiled magnanimously at his beguiling patron. "Colette, this is Ella Jacobs, an American teacher from Florida. She's studying art in Montmartre. And creating couture to display in my shop."

He didn't introduce me as his girlfriend. Does he want Colette to think I'm just an employee?

"Enchantée," Colette purred, deigning to offer Ella the tips of her impeccably manicured fingers. Perfunctory politeness complete, she dismissed Ella with disinterest and returned to lavish her attention on a doddering Jean-Luc. "I'm delighted with today's progress," she effused, offering him a slim, elegant hand. As he escorted her to the exit and gallantly opened the

door, Colette flashed him a blindingly brilliant smile. "Until tomorrow, Jean-Luc. *À demain.*"

Breath caught in her throat, Ella watched Jean-Luc's appreciative gaze follow Colette's perfect ass down the quaint cobbled stone street.

Admiration sparked in his electric eyes. "Her portrait will be perfect. *L'Art de la Danse.* The keynote piece of the entire exhibit. And the highlight of my career."

He turned abruptly and dashed up the stairs. "I have to hurry," he shouted over his shoulder. "I'll grab something to eat at the *tablao.*" A whirlwind of animated enthusiasm, he grabbed his satchel, kissed her brusquely, and disappeared out the door.

Ella tried to dispel her nagging doubts as she diced ham and grated *gruyère* cheese for her *omelette au jambon.*

Colette Ducharme was a knockout. Ella—with her barely-there breasts and slender hips— couldn't begin to compare with those voluptuous, dangerous curves. Colette was beautiful, wealthy, powerful, influential… And she could make Jean-Luc a star.

He won't be able to resist her. With a body like that, how could he? You saw the way he looked at her. He'll lose interest. Just like Paul. It's only a matter of time.

Chiding herself for self-pity instead of rejoicing in Jean-Luc's success, Ella ate her omelet. Cleaned up the kitchen. And finished her custom couture.

She glanced at the clock again. It was past two thirty. Jean-Luc always came home before eleven on the nights he performed. The show ended at ten. Where could he be?

A key rattled in the lock, followed by heavy

footsteps on the stairs.

Ella rushed to open the double French doors as Jean-Luc staggered in. The pervasive odor of alcohol wafted throughout the room. "Where were you?" She hated sounding like a shrew.

"At *Loca Luna*," he exhaled, the fumes nearly choking Ella. "Colette came to the *tablao*... with Olivier and Guillaume. I told everyone about the exhibition." His speech was slightly slurred, and he wobbled on unsteady feet. "They took me out to celebrate after the show." He grinned sheepishly. "I'm plastered."

Ella helped him to the edge of the bed, sat him down, and removed his boots, jeans, and shirt.

He mumbled an incoherent thank you as she laid him down, tucked the sheets around his shoulders, and kissed him softly goodnight.

She crawled into bed beside his warm, naked body. Wrapped her arms around his broad, brawny back. And, desperately trying to ignore the venomous voice of doubt hissing through her mind, gazed through the arched windows to the starry night sky.

Chapter 8

Walking a Tightrope

In the morning, Jean-Luc awoke with a wicked hangover and stumbled into the shower while Ella made fresh coffee. When he came into the kitchen, he declined the juice, croissants, and *confiture* she had artfully arranged on the countertop. He settled onto the barstool, clutched his head in his hands, and moaned softly in pain. With a weak smile, he gratefully accepted the *bol de café*.

"I need to pull myself together," he joked, as Ella refilled his coffee. "Colette will be here soon."

A sickening wave of jealousy washed over Ella. *Stop it. This is an incredible opportunity for Jean-Luc. Be happy for him. And quit thinking of yourself.*

He gulped down his coffee, donned a black T-shirt and faded jeans, and tied back his long, thick hair.

Ella gazed lovingly at the dark tendrils and the curved tips of the scorpion pincers twining up his corded neck. *I want to trace his tattoo with my fingers. And my tongue.* As heat flooded Ella's inner core with tantalizing images of a sumptuous afternoon making love, a knock at the door of the atelier interrupted her sensuous reverie.

With a quick kiss and a whispered goodbye, Jean-Luc disappeared down the stairs.

Disappointed and dejected, Ella cleared off the

counter, washed the few dishes, and spent the afternoon creating couture. But, despite her best efforts to concentrate, venomous visions of Colette Ducharme seducing Jean-Luc poisoned her thoughts.

I'll seduce him myself. She leaves at three, and Jean-Luc doesn't have to work until five. That gives us two glorious hours together…

Ella waited until she heard the door close, then slipped downstairs. Jean-Luc was at the atelier sink, cleaning his brushes and storing supplies. She came up behind him and wrapped her arms around his waist. "How did it go?" she asked brightly, determined not to show the insecurity that gnawed at her gut.

He washed his hands, dried them on a clean towel, and turned to greet her with a huge grin. "Very well," he beamed. "It'll be tough to finish by the deadline, but I'll find a way." A glint of desire sparked in his eyes as he noticed Ella's short, silky dress. His gaze lingered on her long, bare legs before settling on the erect nipples which poked through the soft fabric.

Stroking them with curved thumbs, he made Ella moan as the throbbing and wetness between her thighs became unbearable. He lifted her dress up over her shoulders, set it down on top of the sink, and suckled Ella's swollen nipples until her knees buckled under her weight.

"In here," he gasped, half carrying her to the black velvet couch. "I need you *now*."

He laid her down on the sofa, spreading her legs wide to feast with ravenous eyes as he threw off his shirt and unzipped his fly. His erect cock sprung forth, bobbing in the air, as he kicked off his jeans and knelt between Ella's trembling thighs.

She watched as he rubbed the thick head between her slick folds, spreading the moisture over her sensitive, aroused bud. The soft, slippery skin sent shivers of delight deep inside her quivering quim. She scooted down further on the sofa, enveloping the tip of his shaft with lush lower lips, desperate for him to enter her.

With a guttural growl, he lifted her hips. Wrapped her legs up over his shoulders. And plunged deep inside.

In this position, his pounding pummeled her, his powerful limbs pinning her in place. The relentless stab of his thrusting shaft pierced her with pleasure that bordered on pain, her twitching muscles tightening with increasing tension until she shattered and convulsed under him. With a deep, feral grunt, he heaved himself into her hilt, erupting in plumes of volcanic release.

Breathless, quavering from exertion, they lay still, limbs entwined.

"I needed that," Jean-Luc whispered hoarsely into the shell of her ear, kissing her tousled hair. He withdrew from her embrace, her body releasing his with a soft, sucking slurp.

"As much as I hate to leave, I need to set up on *la Place du Tertre.*" He handed her a clean towel, then wiped himself off when she was done.

While Jean-Luc pulled on his jeans and shirt, Ella slipped back into her dress. "I'll make stir fry for dinner," she said with a contented smile. "So you can eat before you go."

He pulled her close and hugged her tight. "Tomorrow's Sunday. Let's spend the whole day in bed."

Ella's spirit soared like a lark in the summer sky.

****

July rolled into August, with Jean-Luc working each afternoon and every Saturday with Colette Ducharme. Ella kept busy with her English lessons and custom orders for Renaissance Denim Couture, battling the bitter jealousy that sickened her soul. She knew Jean-Luc was under tremendous pressure to complete the portrait—which had to be perfect—and that he was struggling to finish a few additional pieces in time for the impending press conference and publicity shoot. Faced with the rapidly approaching deadline, he worked late into the night, even sacrificing their Sundays together as he raced against the clock.

The second week of August, Ella received the long-awaited notification that her application for an extended visa had been approved, granting her permission to remain in France for an additional six months. She waited until Wednesday—the one weeknight Jean-Luc did not have to work—to share the wonderful news.

They celebrated with a delectable dinner of poached fish and fresh greens at *La Maison Rose*. Pensive, Ella sipped her glass of *Meursault* as she considered her future. "My lease is up in November, so I'll need to fly home one way or another. If I decide to renew it, I'll need to sign the paperwork. If not, then I'll need to move my things out of the apartment. I have to give my landlord at least thirty days' notice in writing before I do—which would mean mailing him a letter now, so he receives it by October 1st."

Jean-Luc reached across the table and took hold of Ella's hand. "I'll fly home with you." An enthusiastic grin stretched across his handsome, bearded face. "*La Fête des Vendanges* will be over, and things will be back to normal." He savored a swallow of the exquisite white wine. "I'll take time off from the *tablao*, give François my nights on *la Place du Tertre*." Dark eyes danced deliciously with hers. "I'll help you move your things out of the apartment. Get to meet your parents and your brother. Then we'll fly back to France. Take a trip south to Perpignan— so you can meet my mother. And celebrate Christmas in Montmartre."

Ella's breath hitched, her heart nearly bursting with joy. *He wants me to stay! He wants to come home with me, meet my family. And he wants me to meet his mother. I've never been so happy in my entire life!* Tears blurring her vision, she squeezed his calloused hand. "I would *love* that," she choked with a sob.

When they returned to the apartment, they sat at the computer beneath the portrait of Ella clutching the bouquet of pink roses. "*Ma Rose Bohème,*" he murmured with a nostalgic smile. "God, how I love looking at you." He raised her hand to his lips, planting a soft kiss on her fingers. The bristles of his mustache tickled her skin.

Together, they rescheduled her return flight to Florida. Purchased Jean-Luc's ticket. And one for Ella to come back to France.

The following day, while Jean-Luc gave his art lessons, Ella walked to the post office and mailed the official letter to her landlord. She requested signature confirmation and a return receipt, proving that she'd complied with the terms of ending her lease. Like a songbird unfurling its wings to take flight, Ella soared back to the *Atelier des Lumières*.

****

Jean-Luc had just finished his art lessons and was working on the downstairs computer when Alphonse entered the atelier. He rose to his feet and extended his hand. The grim expression on his landlord's face sent a shiver of foreboding down Jean-Luc's spine.

"Bonjour, Jean-Luc." Alphonse shook the proffered hand. "I'm sorry to bring bad news." Deep lines creased his forehead, and his eyes were filled with pain. "My mother has had a stroke, and the prognosis is not good. I must sell the atelier as quickly as possible. Fortunately, I have an anxious buyer." Compassion and conviction blazed in his bitter eyes. "I need you to vacate by October 1st. I know the timing couldn't be worse, with *la Fête des Vendanges* the following week, but I have no choice." He withdrew an envelope from the inner pocket of his jacket and unfolded a document onto Jean-Luc's table. "Please sign this as proof that I have given you the required thirty days' notice. I'm sorry, Jean-Luc. My hands are tied."

In stunned silence, Jean-Luc scratched his signature across the form and numbly accepted the copy Alphonse provided.

"I wish things were different." He sighed, tucking the folded document back into his pocket. With a halfhearted smile, he shook Jean-Luc's hand. "Best of luck with the upcoming exhibit." Head bowed, he slipped quietly out the door.

Cottony white clouds floated across the cerulean sky, the leafy trees of Montmartre swaying in the soft summer breeze. Slumped in his chair, the wind knocked out of him, Jean-Luc stared sightlessly out the window. In stark contrast to the perfectly brilliant day, he was bereft and empty, his life suddenly careening out of control.

Ella had received the extended visa. They'd rescheduled her flight. Jean-Luc was going home with her to move out of the apartment. She'd mailed the letter to her landlord. To be received by October 1ˢᵗ. The same day he now had to vacate the atelier.

What an ironic twist of fate. He'd finally convinced Ella to stay. And now he had no home to offer her.

He hung his head in his hands.

He was walking a tightrope with Colette Ducharme, his professional life suspended in delicate, precarious balance. One wrong move, and he would plummet. To the death of his artistic career.

Colette was sexy and seductive. Bold and beautiful. A polished, pampered princess who always got what she wanted.

And what she clearly wanted was Jean-Luc.

For her portrait, she'd chosen a white diaphanous gown to drape over her nude body in an elegant, ethereal pose. With one arm unfurled upward like the delicate wing of a swan, her arched torso curved back over a gracefully extended, elevated leg and pointed toe, Colette resembled an ephemeral fairy. An angelic goddess. The essence of *L'Art de la Danse*.

So far, he'd artfully dodged her overt amorous advances. Politely declined the dinner invitations with implications that they would end up in her hotel. Ignored how she tautly pulled the sheer fabric of her gown over bare, voluptuous breasts when they paused for brief breaks during each session. But now, with the deadline for completion of her portrait rapidly approaching, Colette was becoming more desperate. Daring. And determined.

She was used to manipulating men, like marionettes dancing on a string. Fawning all over her. Falling at her pretty, powerful feet. Available at her beck and call.

Yet the more she tried to seduce him, the more she repulsed Jean-Luc. He didn't want Colette—he wanted Ella. His bohemian rose. His Muse. His heart.

Images of Ella flooded his thoughts.

Blonde hair cascading to her waist like a wondrous waterfall of gold. Slender torso and the long, lithe limbs of a graceful dancer. Gentle soul and generous nature, with an exuberant zest for life. Creativity, intelligence, and a bohemian spirit. And a fiery, intense passion to match his own.

Jean-Luc tossed his hair over his shoulder, shaking himself out of his reverie. He couldn't tell Ella about losing the atelier. He'd have to figure something out. And fast. But, in the meantime, Colette would be arriving soon, and he needed to prepare.

Next week marked the press conference and publicity shoot. Colette was undoubtedly expecting several more portrait sessions. Several more opportunities to seduce Jean-Luc. But he would tell her this afternoon that tomorrow would be their last session.

He was done with Colette Ducharme.

"I'm pleased to inform you that the portrait will be finished tomorrow," Jean-Luc announced with a professional smile at the end of the session. "I'll deliver it personally to the museum Friday afternoon at two." From the corner of his eye, he observed Colette's face fall as he collected his paintbrushes.

"So soon? I thought we wouldn't be done until next week." A hint of desperation tinged her tight voice. She turned toward Jean-Luc, dropping the corner of the gauzy fabric to expose a full, rounded breast.

Jean-Luc averted his gaze, focusing on the brushes in his tightly clenched hand. "The portrait will be completed a week in advance. Well before the deadline." With an exaggerated semblance of hurry, he assembled the various paints and brushes, noisily gathering supplies in his arms and heading toward the exit door. Nodding his head in a polite goodbye, he said cheerfully, "You must excuse me, Colette. I have another appointment. I'll see you tomorrow at two."

****

The following day, Jean-Luc left dance rehearsal at the *tablao* and impulsively decided to walk along the *Allée des Brouillards* where the Impressionist painter Renoir had once stayed. As he strolled through the lush vegetation of the abundant trees, he remembered bringing Ella to this quiet oasis in the center of Montmartre where he'd always wanted to live.

Lost in his thoughts, he nearly missed it entirely. But there, in the walled courtyard of a lovingly restored *Belle Époque* apartment building, was a sign that read: *À louer.* For rent.

Jean-Luc's heart hammered in his chest.

He dialed the phone number of the realtor listed on the sign, and she agreed to meet him on the premises in half an hour. While waiting, he admired the elaborately scrolled design of the wrought iron decorations outlining the three large display windows on the ground floor of the front façade. On the second story, the same pattern of wrought iron enclosed the balcony above the entrance door. Jean-Luc ambled over the grounds, noting the dense foliage of privacy hedges and verdant trees which provided shelter and shade. And covering the trellis in the walled garden behind the beige building, a profusion of fragrant pink roses perfumed the summer air.

Pink roses for Ella. Ma Rose Bohème.

When the realtor arrived, she showed him the trio of spacious workshops behind the wrought iron enclosed windows on the ground floor. Two large closets with numerous shelves offered plenty of storage. There was a private toilet for potential clients. And a deep sink, perfect for cleaning paintbrushes and art supplies.

An elaborate stairwell led to the three-bedroom apartment on the upper level. Behind the open living and dining room area was a large bedroom and private bathroom with a balcony overlooking the rose garden. Along the corridor behind the kitchen was a second bathroom, with two more bedrooms at the end of the hall, one with the balcony jutting over the front door.

It was positively perfect.

"If you are interested in this apartment, I suggest making a deposit today. With this ideal location, it won't last long." The smartly dressed realtor smiled at Jean-Luc as she checked messages on her phone.

"I'll take it. It's exactly what I want." Jean-Luc paid the security deposit and required advance rent, grateful that he'd saved a good portion of his father's inheritance. He completed the application for the lease and waited while the realtor entered the information on her laptop and submitted it for approval. A few minutes later, he enthusiastically shook the realtor's hand. Tucked the key to the new apartment into his jean pocket.

And returned to the *Atelier des Lumières* for the final portrait session with Colette Ducharme.

Chapter 9

L'Atelier du Coeur

Ella strolled along the cobbled stone street, the warm kiss of the sun on her face, her arms as full as her joyous soul. Not only had she found the perfect vintage denim and antique lace for the couture creation, but today was Jean-Luc's last portrait session with Colette Ducharme.

Although he still had a few paintings to complete for the *L'Art de la Danse* exhibit in October, he would no longer be spending every afternoon and all day Saturday with Colette. He'd have time for Ella again. They'd have the whole month of September. She'd be with him for *la Fête des Vendanges*. And share in his triumphant success.

It was nearly four-thirty. The session with Colette ended at four, so Jean-Luc would be in his atelier, cleaning his brushes and putting away his supplies. Ella couldn't wait to show him the beautiful lace she'd found—for the Renaissance Denim Couture creation she'd make, to wear to the publicity shoot. He'd asked her to be at his side, and she wanted to wear something chic, artistic, and trendy.

She slipped into the atelier and tiptoed down the hall toward the open studio door. Jean-Luc would love the lace. It was the same mauve pink as the roses in the portrait he'd painted of her. *Ma Rose Bohème*. His bohemian rose.

Ella burst into the room to surprise him.

And there, in all her nude, nubile beauty, stood a stark naked Colette Ducharme. With Jean-Luc's hand caressing the curve of her plump, perfect ass.

One of Colette's elegant hands rested affectionately upon his, guiding it across her voluptuous skin. Her other arm snaked up behind Jean-Luc's neck to stroke his head, fingers raking through the thick, dark locks of his glorious black hair.

A fierce, ravenous hunger blazed in Jean-Luc's impassioned eyes.

The bags in Ella's arms dropped to the floor.

A piercing cry like the wail of a wounded lark tore from her throat. She spun on her heels, raced down the hall, and bolted out the door.

She couldn't breathe, couldn't think. She ran like the wind. desperate to escape the blinding, searing pain.

"Ella… *come back*! It's not what you think!" Jean-Luc's booming voice bellowed from behind.

She ducked into a *tabac* and hid among the magazines as Jean-Luc went barreling by. Legs shaking, stomach twitching, she shivered, chilled to the bone.

You knew it would happen. How could he resist her? Big boobs, plump ass, gorgeous face. She's rich, powerful… perfect. What can you offer him? Nothing. But she can make him a star.

The shopkeeper eyed her with a mixture of concern and suspicion.

Ela realized she was sobbing. And, with her stomach heaving, was about to puke. She dashed out the door just in time to retch into the grass beneath a tree. She wiped her mouth, straightened her back, and searched her surroundings to make sure Jean-Luc wasn't lurking nearby. No sign of him. She exhaled in relief, trying to calm her shattered nerves.

She wandered aimlessly, lost in grief. She'd been so overjoyed to get the extended visa. She'd wanted more than anything to stay in Montmartre with Jean-Luc. But she'd been a fool to think he'd fall for someone like her. Not when he could have Colette Ducharme.

A smothering weight compressed Ella like a tightly clamped vice. She needed to fly home to Florida. She couldn't face Jean-Luc. She had to escape. Tonight.

Today was Thursday. His night to sketch on *la Place du Tertre*. He'd be there at six, so she'd wait until seven. She had a key to the apartment… which was in her purse! And she'd dropped it on the floor with her bags.

When she'd seen Jean-Luc cupping Colette's perfect ass.

Staggering jealousy stabbed Ella's wounded heart.

She'd get into the apartment somehow. Even if she had to break a panel of glass in the front door. Her passport was in the zippered compartment of her suitcase. And her wallet and debit card were in her purse.

From the upstairs computer, she'd book a flight home tomorrow. Reserve a hotel room. Pack her luggage. And take the RER line to the airport.

Satisfied with her plan, Ella just had to wait until seven. When Jean-Luc would be at *la Place du Tertre*. She took a deep breath, exhaled through her mouth, and wiped the hot tears from her cheeks.

****

Jean-Luc's pulse thundered, his breath heaving, as he stopped running and searched the crowded streets for

Ella. He'd lost sight of her and had no idea where to look.

He couldn't believe what had just happened.

In the studio, he'd just finished Colette's portrait. She'd gone behind the partition to dress, while he cleaned his brushes, capped his paints, and put away his supplies. But, instead of donning her clothes, Colette had emerged buck naked.

For a full-scale frontal attack.

She'd placed his hand on her ass, holding it in place with her own, sliding it all over her curves. With her other hand, she'd clamped his head, pulling his face down for a desperate kiss.

He'd been livid, paralyzed with fury. And—just as he'd started to pry Colette off him—Ella had walked in.

Her exuberant face had fallen in shock. All the light had dimmed in her eyes. Her mouth had dropped open in disbelief as the packages fell to the floor. And the mournful wail from her wounded soul had pierced him right through the heart.

He'd chased after her, racing down the sidewalk. But she'd disappeared. And now, he stood gasping for breath on the street corner, blinded by rage and despair. He couldn't lose Ella. He had to find her. But where could he even begin?

She has to go back to the atelier—her purse is lying on the floor. With no money or debit card, she can't go far. She'll go back to get it. And I'll be there when she does.

Jean-Luc sprinted back to the atelier, immensely grateful to find that Colette had gone. He called his colleague François, and—with a brief explanation that he had a crisis to handle— relinquished his night to sketch on *la Place du Tertre*.

Adrenaline coursing through his veins, tense muscles twitching and lurching, Jean-Luc paced the floor of his apartment, his eyes glued to the cobbled stone square beneath the window outside. Where Ella would have to appear.

****

The clock in the store window showed that it was ten past seven. Jean-Luc would be at *la Place du Tertre*, so Ella headed back to the apartment.

Relieved that it was unlocked, Ella quietly entered the atelier.

She glanced lovingly at the vibrant paintings of flamenco dancers on the walls of the studio, moved to tears at Jean-Luc's extraordinary talent that she would no longer be able to share. In the corner window, a mannequin displayed her latest couture creation— a funky, feminine blend of distressed denim and exquisite antique lace. *I was just beginning to recruit customers. And my English classes were going so well...* Ella swallowed an enormous lump in her throat and stoically climbed the stairs.

The setting sun streaked the sky in vivid shades of violet, pink and mauve, casting slanted rays of gilded light over the sumptuous black bed. Her stomach clenching at the memory of so much passion shared with Jean-Luc, Ella stood transfixed, immobilized with pain.

"I'm glad you came back." Jean-Luc's deep voice reverberated into her bones.

She spun toward him, stunned that he wasn't at work, stung by his bitter betrayal. "I just came to get my things." She tried to shoulder past him, but he pulled her into his arms. She struggled in vain to break free, moaning in pain, tears streaming down her face.

"Please listen, Ella. It's not what you think." He lifted her chin so she would look at him. Anguish blazed in his dark, desperate gaze. "Colette has been coming on to me for weeks. I've been dodging all her advances—showing her I'm not interested, without insulting or offending her. So I wouldn't jeopardize the exhibition."

Ella lowered her eyes from his intense, impassioned face.

"Today was our last session, and she got desperate. Instead of getting dressed to go home, she came out from behind the partition totally nude—and caught me off guard. She grabbed my hand, put it on her ass, and tried to pull my face down for a kiss. That was when you walked in. Just when I was peeling her off me." He bent down to look into her eyes. "Please believe me, Ella. It's the truth."

She desperately wanted to believe him, but doubt sickened her. "She's everything you could ever want. And she can make you a star."

Jean-Luc choked with emotion. "I don't want Colette Ducharme, Ella. *I want you.*" He clutched her hands to his chest like cherished treasure, lowering full lips on them in a tender kiss. "You're my Muse, Ella. My *heart.*" Dark eyes pierced her very soul. "Since you came into my life… my art is more vibrant, my dance more intense. Your passion enhances everything I do. Everything I see and feel. Please don't leave me, Ella. *I can't live without my heart.*"

She flung her arms around his neck and buried her nose into the dark hair at the base of his throat. "I don't want to leave, Jean-Luc. No man has ever made me feel the way you do."

"Then don't go. Stay here, with me." He gently

lifted her chin and swallowed her lips with his own. "Tomorrow, I'm going to *le Musée de Montmartre* with Colette's portrait. She paid for it, and I'll deliver it in person to complete the transaction. I want you to go with me, Ella. Because I'm going to tell her that I'm out. That I don't want to be the featured artist. They can find someone else. Reschedule the press conference. I don't ever want to see Colette Ducharme again."

Ella melted in his arms.

His warm mouth sought hers, tentative tongue parting her lips slowly, waiting for permission to enter.

Ella opened wide to welcome him in.

As his probing tongue delved deep, dancing deliciously with hers, his hands were everywhere—caressing her hair, her back, her ass. He slipped her tank up over her arms. Yanked her skirt down her hips. And moaned as he slid her panties to the floor.

She watched him throw off his clothes, feasting her eyes upon the rippled, tattooed flesh. Her fingers stroked the dark hair across his chest and traced the trail down his taut stomach. His erect cock begged for attention, so she twirled the tip of her tongue around the engorged, swollen head.

He groaned, raised her to a stand, and plundered her mouth with skilled lips as he edged her back to the bed.

Ella's trembling legs gave out.

Jean-Luc laid her down. Kneed her thighs apart. And impaled her.

Wrapping him with arms and legs, she pulled him in deep, clenching tightly inside and out, as if she'd never let him go.

He arrowed into her. Cried out her name. And filled her with liquid flame.

After a while, they dressed and had dinner at *la Maison Rose*. Candlelight glinting in his eyes, Jean-Luc smiled enigmatically across the white tablecloth. "Tomorrow, after we deliver the portrait to the museum, I have something to show you." He raised her hand to his lips. "Something I know you'll love."

"You won't tell me what it is?" Ella finished her glass of *Meursault* and leaned forward in her chair.

"It's a surprise." His dazzling grin took her breath away.

The following morning, while Jean-Luc gave his art lessons, Ella slipped out to buy sandwiches and fresh fruit for lunch. When she came back to the atelier, a small package arrived for Jean-Luc. She glanced at the label. *Au Temps Jadis.* Of Time Gone By.

I wonder what Jean-Luc bought in an antique shop? It's too small for a picture frame or lamp. Maybe this is the surprise he wants to show me later. Ella's heart fluttered in anticipation.

They finished the sandwiches, then went downstairs to the studio.

Ella's stomach clenched as they approached the door where she had stumbled upon Jean-Luc and a naked Colette Ducharme.

As if he'd read her thoughts, he squeezed her hand as they entered the room. He indicated the large canvas which stood on the easel. "This is the finished portrait."

Colette's head and torso were bent back into a graceful arch, with one of her arms curled upward and a leg lifted high off the floor. Gossamer white fabric draped over her body like silken feathers, as if she were a swan soaring through a cloud.

"It's breathtaking," Ella whispered, her fingers

flying to her lips. "You've captured *L'Art de la Danse*. Graceful strength… subtle sensuality…ephemeral beauty." She spun toward him, mouth agape in awe. "It's perfect. Your talent is incredible."

He smiled modestly, pleased with her praise, and wrapped the canvas in protective cloth, tucking the edges carefully under his arm. "Let's deliver this to the owner. And be done with Colette Ducharme once and for all."

****

Fruit-laden vines ripened in the hot summer sun as Ella and Jean-Luc climbed the steep slope of *le Clos de Montmartre* and entered the museum.

Filtered light from a wall of windows illuminated the cheerful foyer where several paintings were displayed on the wall opposite the entrance. Doors along a corridor opened into rooms housing various collections of art, and a wooden staircase led to the second floor for additional exhibits. At a cherry wood table in a room adjoining the entry, Colette Ducharme and two gentlemen poured over paperwork in an ongoing conference. They looked up as Jean-Luc and Ella walked in.

A thin man with sandy hair and glasses smiled in obvious recognition and approached with a welcoming, outstretched hand. "Bonjour, Jean-Luc. Colette mentioned that you'd be delivering the portrait today. We're all most anxious to see it."

Jean-Luc introduced Ella to Olivier, who led them into the conference room and gestured to an empty easel in the corner beside the table.

While Jean-Luc set the painting upon the wooden stand, Olivier presented Ella to his colleague Guillaume and a clearly perturbed Colette.

Ella avoided her disdainful, condescending stare.

Jean-Luc unfurled the sheet, revealing Colette's portrait to appreciative gasps and murmurs of praise.

"It's splendid! Perfect for *L'Art de la Danse*. A most impressive piece. Congratulations, Jean-Luc. You've exceeded our expectations." The dark-haired Guillaume turned from his perusal of the portrait and firmly shook Jean-Luc's hand.

Accepting the effusive praise with a humble nod, Jean-Luc cleared his throat and raised a resolute face. "I have an announcement to make. I'm withdrawing from the exhibition. I've delivered Madame Ducharme's portrait, fulfilling my professional obligation. But I no longer wish to have any further dealings with her ever again." He glared at Colette, simmering with revulsion and rage. "For weeks, I endured your unwanted advances, for fear of jeopardizing my professional career." His impassioned eyes found Ella's. "And nearly lost what matters most." He addressed Guillaume and Olivier, both of whom appeared flustered and flummoxed. "Find another featured artist. Best of luck with *L'Art de la Danse*."

Jean-Luc grasped Ella's hand and turned away from the stunned, speechless curators. He led her out of *le Musée de Montmartre*. Into the glorious sunshine of freedom.

"I feel as if a heavy weight has been lifted off my back." Jean-Luc inhaled deeply, closing his eyes as if to savor the fragrance of roses from Renoir's garden wafting on the soft summer breeze. He grinned down at Ella, his face alight with impish delight. "And now, I'll show you my surprise."

He led her along the quaint, familiar street with the

lush canopy of abundant trees. Ella remembered Jean-Luc describing this area as a peaceful oasis in the heart of Montmartre. *L'Allée des Brouillards.* Where Renoir had once lived.

They walked up a stone path bordered by well-manicured hedges and leafy shade trees to a two-story beige apartment building with elaborate wrought iron decorations framing the three large windows on the lower level and the upstairs balcony over the entrance door. To her astonishment, Jean-Luc retrieved a key from his pocket, unlocked the front door, and escorted her inside.

A large, open studio with three enormous display windows and a gleaming pinewood floor welcomed Ella. Intricately carved wooden doors enclosed three rooms on the lower level, with an equally intricate banister along the stairwell leading to the upper floor.

"There's plenty of room for my paintings here," he said, indicating a long wall extending from a corner behind one of the large windows. "And you could display your couture over there." He gestured to the opposite corner near the other two front windows.

"This is large enough for a sewing room, with plenty of storage for your lace and denim supplies." He opened one of the beautifully carved wooden doors to reveal a spacious room with two windows overlooking a walled rear courtyard with a white trellis covered with blooming pink roses.

Ella's pulse accelerated as comprehension dawned.

"We could share this room for lessons on alternate days, like we do now at *l'Atelier des Lumières,*" he said, opening the door to an equally lovely room overlooking the rose garden. "And I can paint in here." He showed her a large, open studio with enormous, elaborately carved ceiling to floor French doors leading outside to the cobbled stone rear courtyard.

Ella was speechless. And shaking with anticipation.

"Let's go upstairs." Jean-Luc grabbed her hand with an enthusiastic grin.

At the top of the stairwell, another set of carved wooden French doors opened onto a foyer where a large arched window offered a beautiful view of the rear rose garden. To the left was an open living and dining room area with a gleaming hardwood floor. Off the kitchen, a cozy breakfast nook overlooked the same walled courtyard from a smaller window on the right.

"Come this way." Jean-Luc led Ella down the hall to a spacious master bedroom behind the living room area. A set of French doors opened onto a balcony overlooking the rose garden, and the suite contained a private bathroom and separate *toilettes.*

Her mouth agape, Ella turned to stare incredulously at Jean-Luc. "Is this apartment *ours*?"

A dazzling smile lit up his handsome face. "*Oui, mon coeur.* It is indeed." He kissed her hand with chivalrous *panache.* "Let me show you the rest." Dark eyes glinting with glee, he led her back across the foyer, down a hall, past a second bathroom and additional *WC,* to pair of bedrooms on opposite ends of the long corridor.

"This room on the left could be our office. We can set up computer areas for each of us." He led her across the hall to the bedroom with the wrought iron balcony which extended over the front entry below. "And this can be a guest bedroom. For when your parents or my mother come to visit."

Jean-Luc brought Ella back through the foyer to the arched window overlooking the rose garden. He took hold of her hands, lowered his lips to bestow a reverent kiss, and raised an impassioned, intense face.

"I was a wreck—walking a tightrope with Colette, trying to reject her without offending her. Struggling to complete the portrait on time. Trying to finish the other pieces for the exhibit." Brows furrowed, he gazed pensively out the window to the trees encircling the courtyard. "Alphonse came into the shop and told me he had to sell the atelier. That I needed to be out by October 1st. You had just gotten the visa and ended your lease. My whole life was spinning out of control." He looked back at Ella, his eyes widened in wonder. "And then, the other day—I can't explain it, but I felt compelled to come here. To walk along the *Allée des Brouillards*. The peaceful oasis where I always wanted to live."

A dazzling smile stretched across his animated, eager face. "I saw this apartment, with a for rent sign. Called the realtor. She met me here and gave me tour. I knew it was perfect for us. I paid the deposit and signed the lease. And now, Ella...*it's ours*."

He pulled her close and wrapped his arms behind her back, ducking his chin to kiss her forehead. "I've always called you *mon coeur*. My heart." With a boyish grin, he said, "I thought... if you like it...we could name our new shop 'Studio of the Heart.' *L'Atelier du Coeur.*"

Ella threw her arms around his neck and stood on tiptoes to plant an enthusiastic kiss on his smiling lips. "I love it! It's perfect. *L'Atelier du Coeur.*"

His expression became somber and serious. "I nearly lost you," he choked, his voice quavering as he held her close. "I love you, Ella. I want to share my life with you." He stepped back and retrieved a small box from the pocket of his jeans.

Ella recognized the name on the label. *Au Temps Jadis.* The package he'd received yesterday. Her pulse hammered in her throat.

Jean-Luc opened the small black jewelry box to reveal an antique ring. Atop an intricate, delicate setting in the shape of an elaborate rose, a dazzling diamond glittered in the golden sun. "It's set in platinum, from *la Belle Époque*. Shaped like a rose, for *Ma Rose Bohème*. With a heart-shaped diamond. Because *mon coeur*— you're my heart."

He dropped to one knee and offered her the diamond ring. "Will you marry me, Ella? I can't live without my heart."

Ella's shaking legs nearly gave out. Spirit overflowing, tears brimming, she cried, "Yes! I love you, Jean-Luc. I desperately want to become your wife."

He rose to a stand, removed the ring from the box, and slipped it onto the third finger of her left hand. Her heart finger. With a curved thumb, he lifted her chin and lowered his full, sensuous lips onto hers. Sealing the promise with a kiss.

****

Three days later, Jean-Luc had just finished his morning art lessons when Ella spotted the two museum curators she'd met the day they'd delivered Colette's portrait to *le Musée de Montmartre*. Jean-Luc greeted them with a firm handshake and a cordial hello as Guillaume and Olivier entered the atelier.

"Bonjour, Jean-Luc," the sandy-haired Olivier responded with a friendly smile. "I noticed your sign in the window. You're relocating… opening a new shop.

L'Atelier du Coeur?"

"That's right," Jean-Luc replied politely. "On the *Allée des Brouillards*. Where Renoir once lived." He regarded the men expectantly, obviously wondering why they had come. "How can I help you?"

"We've come to ask you to reconsider your decision to withdraw from the exhibition," Olivier remarked affably with a conciliatory smile.

Jean-Luc scoffed and shook his head, clearly not interested in the offer.

"Before you refuse," Guillaume interjected, "we wish to inform you that Colette Ducharme has been terminated and her contract revoked. We do not tolerate sexual harassment of any kind, and she will have no further involvement with *la Fête des Vendanges*, *le Musée de Montmartre*, or the *L'Art de la Danse* exhibition." He paused briefly, allowing Jean-Luc time to process the information. "We'd like you to remain our featured artist, with the hopes that we can still hold the press conference scheduled for this Saturday."

Jean-Luc considered the proposition, his expression wary. "You say Colette has been dismissed, and she will have no further association with the exhibition or the museum?"

"That's correct," Olivier responded with an enthusiastic nod. "In fact, as we speak, she is on a plane, returning to *la Côte d'Azur*."

Jean-Luc raised an inquisitive eyebrow at Ella, and she flashed him a breathless smile of approval.

"In that case, I'd be honored to accept," Jean-Luc announced with a generous grin, shaking Guillaume's proffered hand.

"Excellent," Olivier exclaimed as he shook Jean-

Luc's hand. "The publicity will be ideal to promote your new atelier. There is one problem, however." He exchanged a nervous glance with his colleague. "We insisted that Colette take her portrait, since we want no further association of her with the exhibit." He added hesitantly, "We were hoping you might substitute a different painting for the keynote work of art."

Jean-Luc chuckled heartily. "I have the perfect piece. One of the extra paintings I recently completed for the exhibition. Come, I'll show you. Ella—you, too."

He led them from the front showroom of the atelier to his large, open studio.

At the sight of the tufted sofa, Ella smiled inwardly, remembering Jean-Luc painting her nude portrait, with every session ending in passion on that sumptuous black velvet couch.

Sorting through a stack of paintings leaning against the wall, Jean-Luc selected one, carried it across the room, and set it upon the wooden easel before Ella, Olivier, and Guillaume. He gallantly unfurled the cloth covering, revealing a vibrant painting of Ella in a scarlet, form-fitting flamenco dress, the voluminous ruffled fabric below the knees swirling outward in a dramatic, fiery plume. One of her bare arms curled up toward her head, a pair of castanets clenched within her palm. The other hand flung the fiery, flamenco plume of the dress, like the sizzling, scorching trail of a blazing comet across the sky. Ella's enflamed face expressed pain. Or pleasure so intense it engulfed her in flames.

Swirls of long blonde hair curled like flickering flames, and twisting twirls of fire licked at her limber legs.

"I call it *Flames of Flamenco,*" Jean-Luc announced

proudly. "The fiery passion of my Muse." He kissed Ella's hand. "The woman who will soon become my wife."

Olivier broke out in a grin. "Congratulations! Another fascinating announcement for the press conference."

Guillaume inspected the artistic detail of the painting, then turned to Jean-Luc in awe. "This is even better than the portrait of Colette Ducharme. It's ideal for the keynote piece of art. You're an artist who paints flamenco dancers. You're a flamenco dancer yourself. And now, the *Flames of Flamenco* will feature your artistic talent. And your passion for the woman you love. The press will go wild."

Guillaume grinned at Ella. "You must be there for the press conference Saturday, too. They'll want to interview you as Jean-Luc's fiancée. His Muse." He could barely contain his enthusiasm. "We'll want you to be at his side throughout the entire week of *la Fête des Vendanges*. An integral part of the *L'Art de la Danse* exhibition. The model for the keynote work of art."

At the front door of the atelier, Guillaume shook Jean-Luc's hand as he and Olivier prepared to leave. "Decide which pieces you'd like to exhibit and prepare them for transport. We'll send a truck Wednesday to pick them up. Can you meet us at the museum at two? We can arrange the display and go over the details of the press conference. Does that work for you?"

"Wednesday at two it is. We'll see you then." Jean-Luc shook Olivier's hand.

With a friendly goodbye, the two curators left the atelier and headed back to *le Musée de Montmartre*.

Jean-Luc swirled Ella through the air. "I can't

believe it! Colette Ducharme is gone, and I'm the featured artist for *L'Art de la Danse!*" He set her back down on her feet, pulled her against his chest, and crushed his lips on hers. "Let's go to the new apartment. I have a great idea."

The leafy shade trees welcomed Ella as she strolled with Jean-Luc up the stone path to the *Belle Époque* building with the scrolled wrought ironwork around the trio of windows. Inside the apartment, Jean-Luc took her hand and led her down the hall into the large studio with the carved wooden French doors overlooking the walled garden courtyard. A profusion of pink roses in full bloom perfumed the air through the open windowed doors.

On her left hand, the heart-shaped antique diamond glittered in the golden sunlight.

Jean-Luc's smile took her breath away. "I'm so glad you like it."

He pulled her close and crossed his arms behind her back. "What do you think about getting married on the last day of *La Fête des Vendanges?* We could have a wedding on October 10th. On top of the hill, in the vineyard of *Le Clos Montmartre*. Near *le Musée de Montmartre*, where the *L'Art de la Danse* exhibit takes place."

Ella gasped in delight. "I *love* that idea! We could invite my parents… my brother and his wife. You could invite your Mom and your uncle. I love it. Let's do it!"

Jean-Luc motioned for Ella to wait while he walked across the room and retrieved something from a box in the corner. He returned to her side, spreading a fluffy black comforter on the pinewood floor near the open doors, under the bower of fragrant pink roses.

He brushed his full lips over hers, the soft skin

sending shivers down her spine. He removed Ella's black tank top and tossed it aside. Tugged her black gypsy skirt down over her hips, helping her to step out of it. With a seductive glint in his smoldering eyes, he slid his fingers inside her black lace panties and whispered in her ear. "Come, my heart. Right here, under these pink roses. Let's christen the *Atelier du Coeur*."

A word about the author...

Jennifer Ivy Walker has an MA in French literature and is a professor of French at a state college in Florida. Her trilogy, "The Wild Rose and the Sea Raven", is a dark fantasy paranormal romance retelling of the medieval French legend of "Tristan et Yseult", blended with Arthurian myth, fairy tales, and haunting folklore from the enchanted Forest of Brocéliande.

Her novel, "Winter Solstice in the Crystal Castle", is a medieval romance between a feisty, flame-haired French princess descended from Vikings and the solitary knight who suffers an impossible love for her.

"Flames of Flamenco", a novella by Jennifer Ivy Walker, is a passionate romance between an American teacher studying art in Montmartre--the bohemian heart of Paris-- and the fiery dancer who engulfs her in the flames of flamenco.

Please visit the author here:

Website: https://jenniferivywalker.com/

Facebook: https://www.facebook.com/JenniferIvyWalker

Twitter: https://twitter.com/bohemienneivy

Instagram: https://www.instagram.com/jenniferivywalkerauthor/

Goodreads: https://www.goodreads.com/author/show/22671046.Jennifer_Ivy_Walker

Bookbub: https://www.bookbub.com/books/the-wild-rose-and-the-sea-raven-by-jennifer-ivy-walker

Tiktok: https://www.tiktok.com/@jenniferivywalker